The Library of Lost Souls

Meghan Holloway

Published by Meghan Holloway, 2021.

THE LIBRARY OF LOST SOULS

First edition. February 16, 2021.

Copyright © 2021 Meghan Holloway.

ISBN: 979-8201975821

Written by Meghan Holloway.

Table of Contents

IT IS A TRUTH UNIVERSALLY acknowledged that a robot in possession of a soul must be in want of a life partner. Nell, Human-5014 and Second Librarian of the Athenaeum, has clung to that truth for twenty revolutions. The human extinction is in its last phases, and her desperate quest to find the recipient of her husband's soul has finally paid off. She has one request, one hope for reconnecting with the man she lost so long ago.

AFTER MY GRANDFATHER had a heart attack four years ago, I moved in with my grandparents during his recovery. Late in the evenings, as my grandmother slept in her recliner beside him and my poodle sprawled across his feet, he and I would watch movies.

His preference, inevitably and humorously, was Hallmark movies. I worked on the manuscript of *Once More unto the Breach* during the movies, as there is only so much saccharine sweetness I can handle. But one evening, I glanced over at him from the rocking chair older than I am, and I found him silently weeping.

My grandfather was not a wealthy man, but he was a rich one. He was rich in good humor and a boyish grin. His laughter was sly and contagious.

He was rich in an abiding love for the land and a long, hard day of honest work. He was never happier than when he was outside, toiling away at some project, working with his hands.

He was rich in strength. My grandfather was a stalwart figure of a man. When I was a child, I was certain no one was taller or stronger than he. He was a rock, constant and immovable.

He was rich in generosity. He was unsparing in his friendship and magnanimous with his kindness.

He was rich in tales. He possessed the Scotsman's abiding love of stories. A conversation with him was peppered with anecdotes about misjudged amounts of dynamite blowing a hole the size of a truck in the roof of his mother's kitchen, a brother jumping off a bridge to avoid an oncoming train and landing in mud rather than in the river, and his new wedding band almost severing his finger when it got caught in a bolt on an airplane.

He was rich in love. He told me once that he thought he had been blessed more than any other man with the wonderful family he'd been given. A wife he adored, even with her endless "honey do" lists. Sons he was proud of. A daughter he cherished. Daughters in law he treated like his own. Grandchildren and great-grandchildren who were his joy and delight.

That night, when I moved quickly to his side and knelt beside his chair, I asked, "What's wrong? Are you in pain?"

He wiped the tears from his face. My grandmother, whittled to bone by age, her mind made brittle by dementia, snored softly in the recliner at his side.

My grandfather said in a quavering voice, "It's just so beautiful. Love stories are the most beautiful stories."

I thought about that when I carried his urn to the niche in the columbarium at the state's National Cemetery on a clear winter's day after he lost his battle with Covid-19. In a nook covered by an engraved marble slab, his ashes and my grandmother's rest side by side on a hill overlooking a wooded ravine with a river sighing softly as it passes.

This last year has been difficult for everyone, tragic for many. It has been a time of loneliness and isolation, fear and loss. We have an innate pull toward community, and we found ourselves terrifyingly alone and starkly disconnected.

But even as we experienced the frailty of humanity, we also witnessed the resilience and the indomitable human spirit. We found ways to connect with one another, to forge bonds even in hardship, to show kindness to those who are hurting and to those who have laid their lives on the line for the rest of us.

In the dark night of a pandemic, it is easy to plumb the depths of despair and wade into the bitter moats of sorrow and grief, at our personal losses and at our collective suffering. When I finished my latest work in progress, I started writing a story late one evening a month after I had tucked my grandfather's urn into the marble niche. I wrote about grief and loneliness and the anxiety of witnessing the fragile impermanence of our species. But somewhere along the way, I realized that, at its heart, this was a love story. A love story about what it means to be human, about the ways we grapple with isolation and loss, about the bonds we forge.

Because my grandfather was right. Love stories are the most beautiful stories.

for those who loved and lost in 2020

the first chapter

SOULS WERE NOT CATALOGUED by the name of those who had once possessed them. When they were harvested, they were assigned a random serial number. The algorithm of the database ensured all souls were handled equally.

But this was still a library, and even though the database was faultless in its anonymity, the Athenaeum still kept detailed records of every soul it received into the repository. The holographic files were encrypted. It had taken me fifteen revolutions of studying the codes to unravel the information, but I was a librarian. I was nothing if not determined and diligent when it came to the pursuit of knowledge.

"Be honest with yourself," I whispered, drawing the holographic file from its slot.

The hologram catalogue was located in the bowels of the Athenaeum. Even the barest sound of my voice whispered back to me in an echo. I glanced around, even though I knew I need not worry about discovery. I had gained my position as Second Librarian last year by default when my predecessor died. The human extinction had aided my rise from apprentice. Guilt pricked like a splinter whenever I mused that only one more death would give me the covetous position of Prime Librarian.

But I strove to be honest with myself, and the truth was, I would have more than one reason to celebrate if the Prime Librarian met a timely or even untimely end.

And the truth was, this was about more than the pursuit of knowledge. I had spent countless hours over the last twenty revolutions searching through the metadata in the Athenaeum with one specific purpose in mind.

My fingers trembled. The information rippled. I checked the coding again, and this time the image wavered due to the moisture gathering in my eyes. When a blink unmoored a tear, I brushed it from my cheek with the back of my wrist.

I did not even need to decode the encryption to know what was listed under *Soul Merits*. This soul had been enamored with the rich textures of oil paintings, had found immense solace in the weight of a canine companion draped over his lap, had looked forward to the howl of a storm overhead, and had loved the haunting, mournful swell of cello music.

I pressed a hand to my chest. The steady, if swift, rhythm of my heart belied the long revolutions it had felt hollowed and fractured. The knot in my throat grew as I read his name again, and then I skimmed through the metadata until I found the reference.

Citizen 7-24326

I knelt on the cold floor, the strength leaving my knees in a sudden rush that made standing impossible. All this time searching. Now I had a starting point.

"7-24326," I said, pressing my fingers to my lips.

Now I just had to find the individual who had earned the right to my husband's soul.

AFTER TWENTY REVOLUTIONS of searching, I anticipated the quest for the individual who had earned my husband's soul to be just as daunting. Instead, I found myself standing in the decontamination chamber of a living facility in the ninth sector less than a fortnight later.

The scanner did not recognize my bio-signature for the elevator tube, so I was forced to use the stairwell that all buildings were still required to incorporate. I ventured four stories below and followed the long, narrow hall until I reached the last dwelling.

I took a deep breath and wiped my palms on the slick fabric of my jumpsuit. It was standard issue attire, the exact same uniform everyone wore. The nanotech provided temperature control, resisted wear and tear, repelled moisture, and was practically impenetrable while still being lightweight. It did not wrinkle, but I still smoothed the fabric over my hips, checked the closure seam for gaps, and straightened the collar.

I stepped to the side of the door and allowed the scanner to read my retinas.

"Human citizen," a voice intoned. "Identity, Penelope, Human 5014. Designation, Second Librarian." After a moment, the light on the comm turned blue. "Access granted."

The doors slid apart soundlessly. I took a swift step in retreat at the sight that greeted me on the other side of the doors.

"Human. Why do you seek to gain entry in to my dwelling?"

Only when my teeth clicked together did I realize my mouth had been agape.

I had never known a world without robots. My grandmother had told me stories, though, of the revolutions before WWIV. Before the war, machinery had never been humanoid aside from voices in handheld communication devices and home entertainment and defense systems.

She told me of the fear the world felt once the fighting ended after fourteen long revolutions when the robots commissioned to end the war left the battlefield and ventured into the tattered remnants of society.

Once so many humans had killed one another that the robots could no longer discern who was ally and who was foe, these battered, rusted weapons had attempted to assimilate into civilian life.

Cyborgs, my grandmother had whispered. That was what humans called the first ones, and the fear and tension they engendered when returning from the trenches still bearing their plasma cannons had almost started WWV. The unrest and riots had lasted for ten revolutions. Humans had feared the robots sought to be their overseers and destroyers. Perhaps in those days we still had not realized we had sown our own destruction.

I worked with robots on a daily basis, both droid models and civilian models. Their engineering had evolved over the revolutions. Once the robots themselves took over their own production, the manufacturing was standardized across models to ensure efficiency, durability, and productivity. The civilian models were lithely designed to be 1.7 meters tall. The Tivadium robots had engineered possessed a tensile strength twice that of titanium and a greater ability to withstand extreme temperature. It was 45% lighter than titanium and was impervious to corrosion. All robots now were made with Tivadium, and while they did not possess the fragile organic composite of human skin and tissue, they were built with a head, two arms, a torso, and two legs all modeled on the human figure. Humanoid in shape and facial construction, though if one peered closely at the pearlescent silver surface of the Tivadium, he or she could see the blue electrical pulses and whirring of the cybernetics.

They were an absolute marvel, programmed to be courteous experts of whatever task assigned them.

But that was not what stood before me.

"Human," it repeated. "Why do you seek to gain entry into my dwelling?" Before I could respond, it continued and repeated the question in one language after another.

"I understand the universal language," I said quickly, interrupting it in the middle of what sounded like Old Earth's English. "You..." I took another step backward so my neck was not craning back so far. After a lifetime of being able to look directly into a robot's eyes, this was disconcerting. "You're a First Division, Warrior Class."

"Affirmative."

Only its arms and shoulders were made of Tivadium. The rest of its form was constructed of what appeared to be true titanium. The surface appeared dull and scuffed against the sheen of its arms. I knew I was staring, but I could not help it. I did not realize there were First Division, Warrior Class models still in existence. Most had been decommissioned decades ago.

These were the robots of legend that had marched into

battle ahead of their human compatriots. They had been strong enough to withstand the recoil of the plasma cannons soldered to their shoulders. They had been so efficient that once they reached the battlefield, the war that had lasted over a decade ended within two revolutions of their arrival in the trenches. I had not realized just how tall and intimidating two meters was until I was standing before a robot of that size.

The robots who worked under me as apprentices at the Athenaeum had never seemed threatening. My grandmother's stories suddenly made more sense.

I cleared my throat and lifted my right fist to my left shoulder, bowing my head. "It is an honor to meet you, Warrior."

Now that my shock was wearing off, pride crept in. My husband would have been ecstatic to know this was the individual who had earned the right to his soul.

"Do you..." My gaze darted between its eyes. The latest models of robots were designed with eyes, a nose, ears, the slant of cheekbones, and a mouth. The one before me had a face that was humanoid only in the barest sense of having eyes and a mouth. "Do you remember me?" I asked softly.

I flinched as soon as I said it. I had promised myself I would not ask such a foolish question, when humans had long known that consciousness and memory were not passed on with the harvested soul.

"I have never met you, human," it said, and its voice sounded as if it were escaping from some place deep, dark, and hollow. "Why then would I recall you?"

I refused to feel disappointed, and I blinked rapidly to rid my eyes of their sudden burn. "Nell," I corrected.

The robot simply stared at me. Its face almost seemed impassive. I did not know if that was the expression it commanded or simply the default setting on its build.

"That is my name," I said. "Nell." When it still said nothing, I continued. "And you? Do you have a name?"

"I have no need of a name," it said. "Please state your reason for requesting entry into my dwelling."

"May I come in?" I asked. I was careful to keep my expression and tone pleasant and considerate. It was my librarian face and voice. I used it whenever humans came into the Athenaeum and requested time with a specific soul that had not yet been earned.

For a long, taut moment, I thought the robot before me, who looked as if it could withstand a plasma cannon blast straight to the chest without even rocking back on its heels, was going to refuse my request.

Its eyes were so different from modern designs. There was no delineation between sclera, iris, or pupil. It was simply a solid, gleaming surface of black. Even so, I had the prickling sense that the opaque gaze studied me as closely as I studied it. I fought to stand perfectly still and keep my pleasant expression in place.

Eventually, the robot shifted to the side and gestured for me to enter.

I paused and stared up at it. Could the gleam of a soul be spotted in such obsidian eyes? There was no flicker in the depths. I took a deep breath and crossed the threshold.

I PEERED AROUND CITIZEN 7-24326's dwelling, unable to curb my curiosity. There was not much to pique it, I quickly realized.

The dwelling was beyond utilitarian. It was completely bare save for the sturdy frame of a resting bench against the far wall. As I took in the spartan living quarters, it occurred to me that there was no need for a sustenance dispensary or an elimination closet. There was a single closed door leading off of the room, but even I was not so curious as to descend into rudeness and ask what was on the other side.

I stood in the center of the room as the robot gave a command that slid the panels of the door closed. I clasped my hands at my waist so I would not needlessly smooth my jumpsuit, and I did my best not to stare at him. I was not so bold as to take a seat on the resting bench, nor did the robot offer it to me.

When the robot remained silent, I cleared my throat. I had prepared a speech, compelling and reasonable, but as soon as I opened my mouth, those words eluded me.

"Does the name Malcolm mean anything to you?" I asked.

The robot's head tilted slightly to the side. It was such an oddly canine gesture on this behemoth of a machine that I took a step back. I heard a slight whirring sound before its head straightened.

"No," it said. "Should the name Malcolm mean something to me?"

"He was a human male," I said. "Malcolm, Human 4895."

I swallowed and remembered the way his hair had fallen over his forehead, no matter how many times he had pushed it back with impatient fingers. I remembered the dimple in his left cheek when he smiled, and he had done so frequently. "He could study the holofiles of the work of the Old Earth painter, Gustav Klimt, for hours. He would listen to the sound bytes of Edward Elgar's concertos on repeat. Elgar was a composer," I explained. "And Malcolm loved dogs." The laugh that escaped my throat surprised me. "He would have had twenty-seven canine companions had we the room."

Something flickered in the robot's eyes, like an old phosphorus match flaring to life before being snuffed out. Had I not been watching the robot, I would have missed it. But it was there. I was certain of it.

"You use past tense to refer to this human male, Malcolm, Human 4895," the robot said.

"Yes." I glanced at the resting bench. "May I?" When the robot dipped its head in what I assumed was a nod, I crossed the room and took a seat. The bench was far more comfortable than it appeared. I took a moment to settle amongst the cushioned pads before I found my voice again. "Malcolm died twenty-two revolutions ago. The records at the Athenaeum indicate you earned his soul two revolutions later."

The robot crossed the room, and I tensed in surprise as it sat on the opposite end of the resting bench.

"That was many revolutions ago," the robot said.

"Yes," I agreed. There were still moments in the dark of night when I rolled over in bed expecting to encounter a warm body and was met only by cold emptiness. "Malcolm was my husband." I waited for a beat, but when the robot offered no response, I realized how automatically humans offered condolences, even if the grief was not theirs to feel. I shifted until I was angled toward the robot and clasped my knees. "I have a request to make of you. I understand this is quite..." *Forward* would have been the word my grandmother used. "Unusual. But I would like for you to consider it."

"I cannot promise I will do so," the robot said.

I almost laughed at the honesty, but too much rested on this. "I want you to commission a life partner." The words left me in a rush.

The robot tilted its head to the side slightly and shifted on the resting bench until it faced me more directly. My knees almost touched the hulk of metal that was constructed with a joint that hinged the same way my knees did.

"I have no need of a life partner," it said.

"I don't think that's true," I countered, not knowing if it was or not. "Companionship is something all of us crave. None of us want to be alone." Vehemence crept into my voice despite my best efforts. I carefully smoothed my tone. "I've read the contracts every robot signs when the soul they've earned is installed. After a decade of possessing and caring for the soul, you are allowed to commission a life partner."

There was a beat of silence before the robot said, "Affirmative."

I slid the credit stick from my pocket. Currency was used for few things these days. Housing, sustenance, healthcare, clothing... All was viewed as earned if one contributed to society. But there were some things that still had a price.

I placed the credit stick on the padded cushion between us and pushed it toward the robot. "This has more than enough credits to cover the commission."

The robot stared at the credit stick for a moment before directing its gaze back at me. "I have no need of your credits, human."

"Nell," I reminded the robot. "And you do need my credits, because there is another part of this request." I dropped my gaze to my knees, unable to keep my eyes on those dark depths with no point of reference on which to focus. I rubbed my palms over the curve of my joints. They ached now, especially in the mornings during the cold season above the surface. I wondered suddenly at how swiftly time had passed. I had marked fifty revolutions just last lunar cycle.

"Speak," the robot finally said as the silence stretched between us. "Tell me this other part of your request."

I swallowed and straightened my shoulders. I looked at the robot. "I want you to commission a life partner. And when I die, I want your life partner to receive my soul when it is harvested."

I RESTED MY HEAD AGAINST the back of my seat as the hover-rail sped toward the second sector. Robots lived in all ten sectors of the Citadel, and though humans had the right to make their dwellings in any sector, we had clustered in the second.

In all of my reading about our past, I had discovered we always had a tendency to gravitate toward one another, to build our dwellings as close as possible, to call one another neighbor and live within shouting distance from each other. To seek community seemed to be part of our condition.

By the time the Covid-19 pandemic had run its course a century ago, over half the population had been wiped out. The World War that followed fifteen revolutions later had halved the population again. In 2058, when the rumblings of the Fourth World War were sweeping across the globe, the vast oceans were already dead and the forests had burned or been destroyed. The rapidness with which the remaining population declined was startling. By the time the fighting ended, the mass extinction was well underway and most of Old Earth had been razed to the ground.

And while we humans died out, robots continued to be manufactured to replace the disappearing workforce. With only hundreds of us left now, humans were the alien life forms who had destroyed our own planet, while those we created to help destroy our enemies had taken it upon themselves to be the stewards of nature we had never managed to be.

The oceans that had become solid with plastic and refuse

were cleaned. The seas were still dead, but perhaps one day, long after I was gone, life would return.

The earth and sky recovered more quickly than the water. The toxic clouds that had facilitated sealed, subterranean dwellings disappeared, and we humans no longer had to don our gas masks before venturing above. The forests and jungles reclaimed the land, and the only memory of human existence on the surface of the planet was the occasional glimpse of a moss covered ruin.

Governments had fallen, and crime had been eradicated within a decade of the robot population surpassing human numbers. When I was a girl, my grandmother had told me of the days when a woman could not venture through the corridors at night without great caution and risk of being attacked. To hear of such violence was unsettling, and even in these last days of humanity, I sometimes wondered if we had done this to ourselves. Perhaps as much as we sought community, we had never learned to live in it.

If we had ensured our end, the robots had ensured that the world we had left in ruins was beautiful again. And those of us who could appreciate that beauty were swiftly dwindling. There had been no new births in over thirty revolutions. Our souls were the only thing that would live on after the last of us was gone.

I bit back a sigh.

The robot had seemed to stare at me for long moments before standing with a metallic groan of joints.

"I reject your request," it said.

I stood so quickly my head spun. "No," I said. "Wait."

"You will vacate my dwelling now, human," the robot

intoned. There was no change in the pitch or timbre of its voice, but the hair at the back of my neck stood on end when it turned and stared at me with those fathomless eyes.

I did not take my gaze off the robot as I collected my credit stick. "Please." I forced myself to approach the robot directly when it gave the command for the door to open. I would not shy away. To do so would be the epitome of rudeness. It was merely the size and eerie gaze of this robot that made it seem intimidating, I told myself. "Please reconsider."

"I have no need of a life partner," the robot said.

"But you—"

"This is my response to your request."

I clenched my teeth as frustration welled in me and swallowed back my argument. Staring up at the robot, I realized it would hear no more of my plea. And even though it shamed me to judge the robot based on its model, I could not deny the feeling of unease in its presence.

I lifted a fist to my left shoulder and bowed my head. "Thank you for your time."

It dipped its head in a semblance of a nod, and as soon as I stepped across the threshold, the panels slid closed behind me.

Only now, on the hover-rail back to my silent dwelling in the second sector, did I let out a deep breath and roll my shoulders to loosen the tension that had tightened my muscles. I tilted my head back, running my thumb along the curved edge of the credit stick in my pocket.

"This is not the end," I whispered.

It had never occurred to me that the robot would refuse. The data showed that ninety-eight percent of those robots that received a soul commissioned a life partner once they had met the allotted time constraints in their contract.

I pondered our conversation as the hover-rail reached the second sector, and I strode through the sleek corridors until I reached the entrance of my building.

I had moved into my dwelling in this building only weeks ago. My previous residence had been my home my entire life. I had been born there, raised by my grandmother in one dwelling facility, been a wife and then a widow in another. I never intended to leave. But gradually, I noticed that my footfall was the only echo in the halls.

I walked all eight halls one night, searching through the dwellings that opened at my command. They were all empty. No one answered me when I called out, and my *Hello? Is anyone there?* seemed to whisper back at me, bouncing through the endless, empty corridors.

I had nightmares about those hours I spent frantically searching for another resident in my building.

Everyone around me had died, and I had not realized they had gradually fallen victim to the extinction one after another over the revolutions until I was the only one left.

I requested a transfer in dwellings the very next day.

As I made my way down the hall, I paused at the door to each dwelling, straining to hear the inhabitant within. My ears strained to no avail, but I comforted myself with the comm box's green glow of light at each occupied dwelling.

The lights in my home flickered on as the doors parted at my voice-activation. There was little more to my home than Citizen 7-24326's. Just one low table before the resting bench, a nook for the sustenance dispensary, and a bedroom with an elimination and cleansing closet branching off of it.

I had hung the quilts my grandmother made by hand on the walls to add color to the space. She had stitched together colorful scraps of fabric from a time before clothing had become uniform and standard issue. She had made so many throughout her life that I had enough to decorate the walls and cloak my sleeping pad.

I moved into my sleeping chamber and perched on the edge of my pad, drawing the credit stick from my pocket. I funneled almost all of my quarterly stipend into the account linked to this stick. I had saved everything I could for this one dream.

I set the credit stick aside and went through the motions of readying for sleep. I hummed softly to alleviate the quiet. The ringing silence was an unwelcome but constant companion.

the fifth chapter

FOR LONG MOMENTS, I was not certain what had startled me from sleep. I did not think it was a nightmare, but the last vestiges of sleep were difficult to wade through when I was burrowed beneath my grandmother's quilts.

Until the sound came again.

I sat up quickly and moved to press an ear against the wall that joined my dwelling with the one next door. When I heard it once more, I could interpret exactly what it was.

Someone was crying out for help.

I scrambled out of bed, not bothering to exchange my night sheath for a fresh jumpsuit or even don boots before hurrying down the hall.

The retina scanner seemed to take an inordinate amount of time. "Human citizen," a voice intoned. "Identity, Penelope, Human 5014. Designation, Second Librarian." After a moment, the light on the comm turned blue. "Access granted."

"Hello?" I called on the threshold as the paneled doors slid apart to grant me entry. For an instant, it felt as if I were in my nightmare.

This dwelling seemed just as stark and empty as the ones I had discovered frantically searching through the building.

"Help."

The faint thread of sound jarred me. I followed it into the sleeping chamber.

I spotted the small, bare feet on the opposite side of the sleeping pad's raised platform. I hurried across the room and dropped to my knees at the individual's side. My neighbor was a woman, and relief swept over the deeply lined canvas of her face as I knelt beside her.

"I fell," she said in a tremulous voice. "And I was all alone." She continued in a language other than the universal.

I was not certain which language she spoke, but I took her hand carefully. Confusion clouded her eyes.

"I'm here now," I assured her. "Are you hurt?"

She blinked slowly and slivers of clarity returned with each nictation.

"Who are you?" she asked.

"I'm your neighbor," I said, keeping my voice soft. "I heard you crying out. You told me you fell."

She glanced around, taking in her sprawled position on the floor.

"Are you hurt?" I asked.

"I...I don't think so," she said.

I helped her ease into a seated position and studied her as she caught her breath and straightened her night sheath over her knees. It had been a long time since I had encountered a human as old as she. With the right to elect humane termination, I rarely saw anyone so ancient and withered. The last individual I had known of such advanced age had been my grandmother.

She had been adamant that she die when nature deemed it fit for her to do so. There had been so many times I wished I were allowed to make that decision for her when her mind perished from a wasting disease long before her body followed suit.

"Let's get you into bed," I said, draping the woman's arm around my shoulders and wrapping my own around her waist.

She was painfully light and felt heart wrenchingly fragile as I helped her gain her feet and then settled her back on her sleeping pad. I tucked the standard issue blanket around her.

"You're not my daughter," she said.

"No," I agreed. "My name is Nell."

Her throat moved, and her eyes gained a sheen of moisture. "My daughter is gone. Everyone is gone."

I remembered those empty hallways and the echoes of my own calls. "I'm here," I whispered around the growing lump in my throat.

"But you're not who I want." Her eyes were closed, but tears gathered in the outer corners and then slipped free to stream down her temples.

I sat with her even though I was not who she wanted until her tears had dried and her chest rose and fell evenly in sleep.

I escaped from her dwelling feeling as if a hollowness were expanding in my chest. Curled up on my own sleeping pad, I clutched a pillow tightly against me. It did not return my embrace, of course, and no matter how securely I held it to my chest, it did not alleviate the emptiness I felt within.

AT THE ATHENAEUM OVER the next lunar cycle, I studied the robots who worked under me. They worked politely around one another and were courteous and deferential. But none of them sought another out. They did not converse as they worked. They did not cluster together during breaks.

I watched them as I ventured through the corridors on my way home, and while they nodded to one another and to me in passing, none walked together or lingered to share details of their days with each other. I wondered why I had never noticed that they did not have the same tendency toward community as humans.

I have no need of a life partner. That was what Citizen 7-24326 had said to me.

Of course, he would not think he needed companionship when he had never known it. I had assumed that with a soul, it would be an automatic hunger. That was why those who earned a soul were allowed to commission a life partner after the allotted time. But Citizen 7-24326 was one of the first generations of robots. He had been in existence, alone, far longer than he had lived with a soul.

Perhaps he did not even understand what companionship entailed.

I realized belatedly that I was thinking of Citizen 7-24326 as *him*. It was a leftover human tendency to assign gender when robots had not been created as either male or female. Perhaps it was the unexpected size of the First Division, Warrior Class robot, or perhaps it was the fact that my husband's soul resided somewhere in the depths of the machine.

I selected a ration from the sustenance dispensary and curled up on my resting bench to eat the final meal of my day. I pondered the situation, and as I did so, I found myself shortening the robot's name. Citizen 7-24326 was a mouthful.

"I need to show him," I said aloud to the empty room.

How to show him was another matter, and I dwelled on it throughout the night and the next day at the Athenaeum. So much so that I did not see the Prime Librarian approaching until it was too late to evade her.

For revolutions I had tried to dampen the animosity that threatened to choke me whenever I interacted with this woman. But every time I looked at her, I could feel the emotion simmering in the pit of my stomach.

It was immature and senseless, a complete waste of my time and energy. But there it was. I was a woman in her fiftieth revolution who still harbored burning emotion for a girlhood rival. It was not my finest moment, but I had held onto him so long that of course I was still embroiled in bitterness toward her as well.

I sucked in a deep, calming breath when she called my name and pasted on a smile that felt more like a grimace.

"Marissa."

The other woman was taller than me, and her hair was always kept in a neat, smooth coif. She was brilliant and polished, and I had to admit that she had rightfully earned the role of Prime Librarian rather than merely falling into it when a predecessor died.

"May I borrow a moment of your time?" she asked, voice

so solicitous I knew it was not a request.

"Of course," I said.

I followed her through the towering halls of the Athenaeum until we reached her office.

When I was seated across from her, she clasped her hands and met my gaze.

"I am certain after working here for so long that you are aware that everything is closely monitored in the Athenaeum."

"I'm aware of that," I said, voice even.

"Then you're aware that your decryption efforts have been noticed for revolutions now."

I kept my face expressionless. The anonymity of souls once they were harvested was the reason randomized serial numbers were assigned by algorithm. There were no sinister motivations to hiding the identity of the individual who had once possessed the souls. Instead, it was meant to ensure every soul was treated with equal care.

I had long suspected the Prime Librarian was aware of my efforts, but this meeting confirmed it.

I met her gaze without flinching. "Have I done anything wrong?"

She sighed and leaned back in her chair. "I have a feeling you already know you have not. And while I do not have your mind for coding, I can guess by the lack of extra hours you have worked in the last lunar cycle, you've finally found what you were looking for."

"Was there something specific you wanted to speak with me about, Prime Librarian?" I asked, reaching for politeness and deference and perhaps missing the mark.

"Finding his soul will not bring him back," she said. Her

voice was quiet, laced with sorrow and pity.

The last felt like a blow, and I rocked backward with the force of it.

"What good will it do you?" she asked.

My hands trembled as I stood, and I moved to the door without even requesting a dismissal.

"When will you let him go?" she asked. "Don't you think it's time to move on? To *live* instead of trying to reconnect with a man who is long dead?"

I stopped, spine stiff with indignation and frustration. I turned back to her. "Like you did?" I asked, and the venom in my voice was evident to both of us.

She stared at me for a long moment. "Yes. Like I did. I loved him as well. But unlike you, I don't need to find his soul to remember that."

My eyes burned as I left her office. I paused in the hallway and rested a hand against the smooth, cool surface of the wall, needing to brace myself against the emotions that swept through me.

When I could stand without danger of my knees buckling, I left the Athenaeum without bothering to return to my work.

The corridors at midday were quiet. The hover-rail from the fourth sector to the second was almost empty. No voices echoed through the hallways of my building.

But when I approached my dwelling, the door next to mine slid open as I passed.

I paused and met the old woman's gaze. I had not seen her since I assisted her in the middle of the night last lunar cycle.

"Are you the woman who offered me aid?" she asked, voice tremulous.

I had to clear my throat before I could speak. "I am," I said, and because I was not certain how much of our conversation she remembered, I continued. "I'm Nell, your neighbor."

"My name is Donna. Would you like to come in?" she asked.

I glanced beyond her, into her brightly lit home. "I would," I said. My own dwelling waited for me, dark and empty.

She stepped aside, and I crossed her threshold.

the seventh chapter

HER DWELLING WAS AS small as mine, but she too had made efforts to add color to the gray. In the light, I could see the paintings hung on her wall. They were renderings of things I recognized from the holovids of Old Earth. Flowers in vases. Fruit in a bowl. A filmy curtain over a window. A bird on a branch. A bee on a blade of grass.

The paintings were small and simple, but lovely and poignant. Memories of another life in another time, perhaps.

I turned from studying them and found her watching me.

"These are wonderful," I said.

Her bittersweet smile festooned her face in even more wrinkles. "My mother painted those." She gestured toward the resting bench. "Please, sit."

I did so, and she perched near me.

"My memory is not what it once was," she admitted. "But I fear I may have been terribly rude to you the night you helped me. I've been embarrassed to approach you about it."

"Don't be," I said. "I understood."

She reached out and patted my hand. "You are kind, dear, not to hold an old woman's cruel grousing against her."

I stared down at my hand. My skin prickled with warmth where she had touched me. I placed my palm over the spot, desperate to hold onto that bit of contact.

When I glanced up at her, I saw that she was staring at me. There was empathy in her gaze. She slowly, deliberately reached out and placed her small hand over mine.

My throat closed. The pain that grew in my chest felt so real

I thought it would pierce my heart.

"How long has it been for you?" she asked softly.

I had to swallow before I could respond. "Twenty-two revolutions," I whispered.

Her fingers convulsed on mine. "You poor dear."

I turned my hand under her grip until I could hold onto her as well. I had forgotten how warm a human hand was. Forgotten the softness of flesh against mine. Donna's hand felt both fragile and strong around mine. I could feel the delicate structure of her bones. Her palm was worn smooth from age, and the wrinkles on her skin were deep and layered.

"And for you?" I asked.

A sheen of moisture glinted in her eyes. "Three revolutions for me. The last to leave me was my daughter."

"I'm sorry," I offered her, even though it was too little.

She nodded. "As I am." She squeezed my hand. "But, such is life, is it not? A series of triumphs and losses, and at times, one outweighs the other. It seems we are all in a season of loss now." She met my gaze. "It will end soon enough."

A chill crept over me at her words, and I gently extricated my hands from hers. My hand immediately felt cold without the weight and warmth of hers against my skin. I smiled at her. "Hopefully we can still find some triumphs before the end."

I sat with her into the evening as she told me about her daughters and her one grandson, all dead and gone, although still very present in her mind. We shared a meal together, and even though her fatalism sent unease crawling up my spine, her company was better than none.

When she mentioned her family's souls being harvested, her tone turned bitter.

"Will you not donate your soul when it is your time?" I asked carefully.

She scoffed. "It isn't theirs to have. I won't have what's made me *me* leeched away and given to some piece of scrap metal shaped to resemble a human."

I considered her words later as I returned to my dwelling. I had long resigned myself to the mass extinction. There was nothing to be done for it. All the scientific advancements in the world could not save a species dwindling so sharply. Certainly, there had been desperate conservation efforts throughout the last century. Whether it was pollution or dwindling resources, each generation had produced less and less until there were no new generations born. In vitro fertilization failed. The cloning efforts decades ago had seemed successful at first, until a virus manifested in their genes and wiped out every individual created.

After the cloning efforts failed, scientists had turned to the idea of harvesting souls from willing donors at death. It was one last effort at preserving a dying species. We may not survive, but perhaps our humanity would.

It had been met originally with the same disgust and horror my neighbor had shown. But new ideas were always met first with resistance, and the distrust faded over the revolutions as our extinction loomed closer and closer.

Who would not want a small fragment of themselves left behind? Who would not want a splinter of themselves embedded in a future they would not otherwise see?

For revolutions, I had known I would donate my soul, and for decades now, I had sought the place I knew my soul belonged.

I ran my fingers up my arm, over the curve of my shoulder, along the arch of my collar bones. I lay back on my sleeping pad and tugged a pillow over me. It was too light to feel like warm, male weight over me, but if I thought hard enough, I thought I could recall the tenderness in my husband's touch.

I sighed and rolled over, curling my knees toward my chest.

"Lights off," I commanded quietly, and my sleeping chamber was plunged into darkness.

I had spent so many revolutions alone searching for the remnant of the man who had, for a brief moment in time, given me the world in his smile. I had never given up, and I kept digging through the records of the Athenaeum until I found him.

Resolve filled me. I had worked too diligently for too long to be stymied now. One *no* was not going to dissuade me.

I DID NOT HAVE A PLAN as I took the hover-rail to the ninth sector and disembarked at the station closest to his dwelling. It was morning, and the corridors were not empty as they had been when I last visited.

"Are you lost, Second Librarian?"

"Do you need assistance?"

The questions from passing robots were courteous, and I responded in kind. I imagined their curiosity was piqued to see a human wandering through their district when so few ventured beyond the second sector.

The First Division, Warrior Class robot was leaving his dwelling as I turned the corner in his building.

He paused when he spotted me. "Human female."

I thought I could almost hear a hint of frustration in that deep voice. If he were capable, I thought he would have sighed.

I bowed my head. "Citizen 7-24326. Nell, remember? That is my name."

He halted before me but offered no response to my reminder.

"What pronouns do you prefer?" I asked. I did not want to be disrespectful, even in my thoughts toward this robot. "I use she and her."

"I am satisfied with using he and him." He moved to pass me in the corridor, and I hurried after him until he stopped and look down at me. "Why are you here? I gave you my answer to your request."

I clasped my hands and carefully met the First Division,

Warrior Class robot's gaze. I almost regretted not thinking through a plan to approach him, not having a script in mind. Then again, the words I had prepared and rehearsed had flown out of my head the moment I met him.

Do not be afraid of him, I ordered myself. Yes, he was larger and more intimidating than any other robot I had ever come across. He was also far older. I had checked, and every other First Division, Warrior Class had been voluntarily decommissioned and repurposed.

What made him refuse that fate? Was it my husband's soul? I searched his fathomless eyes for any kind of spark, but found only darkness. Was he lonely, the last of his kind? What horrors had he seen on the battlefield?

I shook myself, realizing he was staring at me awaiting my answer.

"I have another request to make of you." I could almost imagine the way he stared at me was the robot equivalent of long-suffering resignation. I cleared my throat. "I would like to spend time with you. You say you have no need of a life partner."

"I do not."

I held up my hand, and from the way his head drew back, I imagined no one had previously had the audacity to gesture for his silence.

"You cannot know what a gift companionship is if you have never experienced it," I said.

He studied me with that endless gaze for a long moment. "You hope to show me companionship and change my mind about commissioning a life partner."

I saw no reason to lie to him. "Yes."

He turned away from me. "My response to your request will not change."

"Please, Seven, I—"

The robot's face swiveled toward me, and I froze when I realized what had slipped past my lips. His head tilted in that startling canine gesture.

"What did you call me?"

"Forgive me," I said quickly. "I meant no disrespect."

"What did you call me?"

I swallowed. "Seven."

"Short for 7-24326?"

I could not tell from that bottomless voice what his thoughts on the nickname were.

"Yes." My voice was hesitant, and I eyed him warily.

"Hm." It was an undeniable human sound he made.

"I apologize. I will not call you that again."

"You may," the robot said, surprising me. "I am not opposed to you referring to me as Seven."

I blinked. My shoulders slumped, and I realized how tense I had become. I kept expecting him to lash out at me, like some untamed beast of old, but there had never been an instance of robot-against-human violence. I was ashamed of my reaction to him.

"My response to your request will not change, but I permit you to spend time with me."

The smile that spread across my face caught me by surprise. "That is very magnanimous of you."

"Affirmative," he said.

I fought the astonishing urge to laugh.

And we'll see about changing your mind, I said silently.

He moved past me down the corridor, and after a moment's hesitation, I followed.

"I am the Second Librarian at the Athenaeum," I said as I traipsed after him.

"I know," he said.

I missed a step at that admission, but then remembered that even if his technology had not been updated with facial recognition, his dwelling comm had announced my name and designation the first time I approached him. "I don't work today, but everyone is always curious to see the Hall of Souls. Would you care to spend the day at the Athenaeum with me? We could also—"

"No," he said, turning down a corridor that ended in a doorway. He leaned forward to allow the retinal scanner to confirm his identity before the doors slid apart to reveal what could only be described as a garage. There were all manner and sizes of hovercraft stored within. "I have a task to attend to, human."

"Nell," I corrected automatically. I stared at the rows of vehicles. "You have a...job?"

"Affirmative."

There were no wars at hand. The skirmishes that had followed the Fourth World War had been violent, but they had long been snuffed out. I could not fathom what a First Division, Warrior Class did for a job aside from fighting, but I would not be so rude as to ask.

Seven must have sensed the curiosity in my silence, though, as we crossed through the garage. His footsteps rang across the floor, and I had to quicken my steps to keep pace with him.

"You may ask," he said. "If you had cogs in your skull cap, I would be able to see them turning."

I laughed outright. "Very well, Seven." I darted a glance up at him, and I thought I saw the set of his face plates shift. I wondered if that was his version of a smile. "What is your job you must attend to?"

His head tilted again. "If you like, I will show you."

I did not even need to consider it. "I would like."

There were hovercraft of all makes parked in uniform rows. He approached one that appeared to be as old a model as he. When he tossed his satchel into the vehicle and climbed aboard, I hesitated.

"Is this airworthy?" I asked.

He made a chuffing sound, like the airbrakes on the hover-rails, and held out his hand to me.

I met his gaze. It was difficult to parse expression from those dark depths, but I thought I sensed a challenge in them.

I caught his hand and allowed him to assist me aboard.

"Have you ridden in a hovercraft?" he asked.

"Not for revolutions," I said.

He dipped his head toward the jumpseat. "Strap yourself in, then."

The vehicle coughed as he fired up the engine, grumbled in what sounded like rebellion, and emitted a series of creaks and groans that had me scrambling with the harness.

I snapped the last buckle in place as the hovercraft lurched into the air. I wondered if my soul were going to be harvested far earlier than I had anticipated.

Seven stood before the controls with his feet braced apart, hands sure on the instruments. Despite the bumpy start, he guided the hovercraft into the elevator tube.

My preoccupation with watching him prevented me from realizing he had not selected the option to descend to the levels of the thoroughfare until we had already begun our ascent.

"We're going above?" I asked, my breath catching in my throat.

Before he could respond, we were at the surface.

I automatically reached for the gas mask that had once hung around my neck constantly. Panic sank jagged teeth into me when my fingers encountered only the collar of my standard issue jumpsuit. The light blinded me, and I squeezed my eyes shut against the piercing brightness.

How many revolutions had it been since I had ventured above? We were allowed. There were no bans permitting us from ascending past the surface.

I could clearly remember the yellow tinge to the air, though. The way it burned my eyes even more painfully than the light. The acrid stench that clung to me even after going through the decontamination chamber.

I could remember the day my mask had formed a leak. The bitter taste on my tongue. The sharp, needling sensation in my throat and nose. The slick of blood over my lips and chin as my nose began to bleed. The desperation that had gripped me when my lungs squeezed tighter and tighter, struggling to find oxygen in the poison I was unwittingly inhaling.

It had taken me numerous lunar cycles to recover from the exposure, and I had never ventured above again. Not even when the alert had gone out five revolutions ago that the air above had become breathable again. I could still remember how it felt to be starved of air, gaping and gasping.

I could not breathe now, I realized. I heard frantic

wheezing, a terrifying whistling sound. I did not realize it came from me until Seven shifted toward me.

"Human," he said, turning from the instrument panel.

My hands were shaking, clinging to my collar, stretching it away from its constriction around my throat.

The robot approached me, and I thought I saw curiosity in his expression.

"You appear to be in the midst of a panic episode," Seven intoned.

I could not draw precious, clean air into my lungs. Heat swept up my chest, and black spots winked at the edges of my vision. Had I not been seated and strapped in, I would have fallen.

My nails gouged my throat as I tugged at my collar. Seven caught my arms and drew my fingers away from my throat. His hand spanned almost the entire length of my arm from my wrist to my elbow. My eyes frantically sought his.

"Listen to me, human female," he said, leaning over until his face blocked out my range of vision. "You are well. You are safe. The above is no longer a danger to your kind. Are you listening to me?"

I nodded my head desperately. I was going to die. I could not get any air.

"Good," Seven said. "Now breathe. Slowly and steadily."

I shook my head. I could not draw breath into my lungs.

He crouched before me. The hovercraft hummed under us. The sun pierced my eyes, and I squinted to keep my focus on Seven.

"The first time I fired my plasma cannons, I was unprepared for the recoil," he said suddenly. "My mass is built to withstand such force, but engineering does little if you are unbalanced and ill prepared. It was my first mission, the first discharge of my weapon on the battle field, and I was knocked right on my can."

I sucked in a startled breath. I focused on him completely, stunned at the amount of words he was stringing together when he had seemed so closed off and nearly monosyllabic to this point. If he did not have a hold of my arms, I would have latched onto him as tenaciously as I clung to that deep, even voice.

He made that chuff of sound again. "Like getting hit with a hover-rail, it was. I could not be mortified for too long, though."

I took another cautious breath and tasted only clean, pure air. "Why?" I managed to croak. And at the same time, I wanted to ask him about his feeling of embarrassment. That was a startlingly human emotion for a being so inhuman. But I did not have enough air to form the question.

He studied me as I gasped for another breath. "Because had I not ducked at such an opportune time, my head would have been blown off by return plasma fire."

Another gulp of air made it into my starved lungs, and the black spots receded from my vision. The band about my chest loosened.

"Ducked?" I wheezed.

"Affirmative," he said. "That is what I told anyone who commented."

My chuckle was ragged, and my eyes were watering at the glare of sunlight. I took a deep breath. There was no pinching constraint in my lungs, no firebrand of toxins in my throat and nose. I squinted and peered at Seven and then beyond him.

The above was so bright it was painful, and I wished I had a pair of tinted goggles to shield my eyes. I palmed away the moisture that streamed from them, a result of the glare and the panic that had almost choked me.

It was not as I remembered it.

I remembered the above cloaked in perilous yellow smog that cloistered the sky and dampened the light from the sun. I remembered dust and how the wind had flung it like shards of glass with relentless gales that stayed at Condition 4 levels with no human structures or forests to buffer their violence. The world had been barren and smoldering. I remembered the lifelessness, as if the planet itself had a soul that had been stripped away.

From what I could see through slitted eyes, the world was not the same. I knew it would not be, of course. I had read the reports and seen the holovids. But to feel the warmth of the sun on my face, to witness a sky so blue it pained me to look at it, to see verdant, if blurred, growth through my streaming eyes was an entirely different experience. To breathe the clean air myself...

I could breathe again, and I was stunned to realize it was courtesy of the robot crouched before me.

It was only when he released my arms that I realized he still held them. He straightened with a creak of joints and moved to his satchel. He retrieved something from his bag, approached me, and offered it to me.

A pair of tinted goggles.

I slipped them over my head and hurriedly grabbed them before they slipped down my face. I pulled them off and adjusted the straps before resetting them over my eyes. I breathed a sigh of relief and looked around without the light feeling as if it were slicing through my eyeballs.

There were trees. True, live, growing trees. Grass that looked plusher than any fiber rug. It was a patchwork of color that reminded me of my grandmother's quilts. The colors after spending so long in a world steeped in shades of gray left me dizzy.

I adjusted the goggles on my face and looked at the robot as he moved back to the instrument panel.

"You need goggles?" I asked without thinking.

"Not for the sun," Seven said. "My ocular hardware adjusts according to the light. But there are still storms that sweep in unexpectedly. Cleaning dust and grit from my sockets is a chore I do not relish."

"Thank you," I whispered. I hoped he knew my gratitude was for more than the goggles.

"Are you ready?" he asked.

"Affirmative," I said softly.

And this time, I was certain that the shifting of his face plates was a smile.

the ninth chapter

I STARED AT THE PASSING landscape. My eyes had finally adjusted to the brightness with the protection of Seven's tinted goggles. I marveled at how many different shades of green existed.

Staring at the passing world as we flew over it, though, made me dizzy. My head began to swim and my stomach lurched. Finally, I was forced to close my eyes and take deep breaths through my mouth to quell the urge to hurl the contents of my stomach over the side of the hovercraft. I could not imagine my companion having much patience for that.

Although he had surprised me. I cracked one eye open and studied his broad back. He had shown me a level of compassion and understanding I had not expected.

Every robot I knew was courteous and considerate, helpful and polite. But he, a weapon of war, had gone beyond that and shown me kindness.

The seam between his original construction and his new Tivadium arms cut a sweeping line on either side of his back from his neck to his lower torso.

I closed the eye I had cracked open, but even with darkness shrouding my vision, I could recall the delineation of grafting. They almost resembled the scars of wings that had been removed.

Eventually, my stomach stilled enough for me to open my eyes again. I kept my gaze straight ahead, avoiding peering to either side of the hovercraft.

The landscape was changing and the air was growing

warmer. The lush forests had dissipated into golden plains where the wind swept over the grasses, bowing the heads in a rippling wave.

The plains gave way to a different type of forest. While the first we had passed through was lush and thick, this one appeared sparse and scraggly in comparison. The greens were muted. The foliage spiked and fragmented.

The smell changed as well. The crisp bite of fresh air untainted by poisonous gas was soon replaced by warmer currents that held a strange odor.

"What is that smell?" I called to Seven.

"Dimethyl sulfide," he responded.

I had been watching the spindly forest dwindle, but at his answer, my gaze snapped to him. The world was so much larger than I remembered before we retreated below ground. It was at once awe inspiring and terrifying. I had never felt so small or so vulnerable.

"Is that poisonous?" I asked.

"No," he said, but tension had already crept over me.

The sparse forest ended suddenly, as if a line had been drawn it dare not cross. There was no grass, green or golden. Instead, the surface of the planet here was carpeted in rolling hills of white.

I unbuckled my harness and crossed carefully to Seven's side as he eased the hovercraft into a descent. This was sand, I realized. I recognized it from imagery of the world prior to pollution, before humans filled the water, shores, forests, and grasslands with our waste.

But I did not recognize what lay beyond the sand.

A surface as still and gray as old steel stretched flat and

listless in every direction. The expanse was overwhelming, and the odor different even from what I had smelled before. The smell here was more pronounced, brackish and stale and putrid.

"What is this?" I asked.

Seven landed the hovercraft and powered it down until it rested in the trough of the waves of sand. He leaped down from the craft in a movement that was surprisingly graceful, even though it disturbed a tremendous amount of sand. He gestured for me to follow him.

I held onto the railing of the hovercraft as I stepped down, clinging to the side when the sand shifted disconcertingly underfoot. When I had my legs under me, I followed him up the crest of a dune and stood at his side.

I lifted the borrowed goggles to confirm the color without the tinting. It stretched endlessly before us, gray and still and smelling of death. It seemed as barren as a desert, but there was a strange sense of movement to the surface, even though at first glance it appeared solid.

"This is the ocean," he said quietly.

I looked up at him. "That cannot be. This does not look anything like the holovids I've seen."

"Those were taken in the time before," he said. "When the life had not been choked by refuse."

It was haunting in its utter stillness when every record I had seen of the ocean showed it to be a mercurial, tempestuous beauty. What lay before us seemed stagnant in comparison.

"All the data says the oceans have been cleaned and decontaminated," I said. "That life may return."

"It already has," Seven said. "Come see."

I followed him across the dunes. The sand shifted and sighed underfoot, making my gait unsteady and precarious. The grains filled my boots and stuck to my jumpsuit. The closer we drew to the water's edge, though, the harder packed it became and walking became less of a struggle.

Seven stopped at the water's edge and knelt, but I hung back, uncertain.

It appeared more like oil than water, viscous and carrying that strange, stale odor as it shifted and sighed against the sand.

He dipped his fingers into the water. After a moment, I heard a whirring and the water around his hand rippled.

"What are you doing?"

"Taking samples to analyze," he said.

He withdrew his hand from the water and tapped his wrist. My eyes widened when a projection of data illuminated the space between us. I studied the code but could make no sense of it.

"This shows there *is* life in the water?" I asked.

He straightened from his crouch and turned to me. "It is an analysis of the strains of microbes found in the sample," he said. "Here is a different view." His fingers moved over the inside of his forearm and the projection changed.

Instead of strings of code, a magnified image of the microscopic organisms collected in the sample appeared. They were various shapes and sizes, squirming and shuddering across the projection.

"Up until the last revolution, this area was a dead zone," Seven said. "I collected samples regularly and found nothing. But then I drew a sample and spotted cyanobacteria."

"Is that what all of this is?" I asked.

He pointed to different microbes on the projection. "Bacteria, archaea, protists. I think this one is a virus."

I took a quick step away from him.

He made a grating sound in his throat. "Do not be alarmed. There were once more viruses in the oceans than there were stars in the universe."

I peered at the projection. "And this means there is life in the ocean." I gestured to the unending gray expanse. "Somewhere out there."

"No," he said. He dipped his head toward the projection. "This *is* the life in the ocean. It means the waters are being reborn. This is its very first gasp for breath."

"That is..." I studied him. His gaze was locked on the microbes darted around the projection. There was only so much emotion metal could convey, but his features seemed alight with excitement and satisfaction. "Amazing."

"I have requested permission to take a watercraft farther out over the water to run additional tests at different depths," he admitted. He tapped a sequence on his wrist and the projection faded. "With the growing amount of microbial activity I have seen in the last revolution, I believe I will be able to find plankton, a crucial food source for aquatic organisms."

I looked out over the water that had seemed so lifeless. "If there is a food source, then there are also likely creatures to eat the food."

"That is my hope," he said. "And if there are no such creatures now, there will be." He held out his arm, the samples he had drawn contained within. "This is the beginning."

"Show me more."

"DO YOU NOT HAVE SOME place to be, human?" Seven asked when he exited his dwelling and found me standing in the corridor a fortnight later.

"Nell," I reminded him automatically. "I have another day away from the Athenaeum."

Over the last two weeks, I had taken off more days than I had worked. Each day, I sought out Seven and accompanied him as he ventured above and collected samples from various bodies of water. I had accompanied him to ponds and lakes, oceans and marshes. In truth, I had spent so many hours at the Athenaeum over the last two decades that I could take an entire revolution off from my duties as Second Librarian, and no one would complain. The Prime Librarian might even breathe a sigh of relief.

"Are we going back to the ocean today?" I asked.

He stared at me for a long moment. "No," he said finally. "To a river north of here."

He did not object when I fell into step beside him as he headed to the garage. He had been a courteous, if distant and perhaps begrudging host each time I showed up at his door requesting to accompany him.

When I climbed aboard his hovercraft, he made that huff of sound like air brakes but fired up the engine. This time, it flared to life with a mere wheeze and hack.

"May I borrow your goggles again?" I asked.

He was offering them to me before I even finished my request.

The sun still blinded me as we took the chute to the above. But today, there were clouds in the sky. Not the dense haze of yellow poisonous gas that had once descended from the sky. Instead, these clouds were soft, curved formations in white that appeared to have weight and substance. They were changeful, taking on multitudinous shapes as we raced over the land.

"Can we go high enough to touch the clouds?" I called to Seven.

He glanced over his shoulder at me and then up before shaking his head. "You would need supplemental oxygen were we to venture so high."

Another time, I promised myself. I drew my gaze from the sky above to the ground below.

Heading north for the first time since I began accompanying him, we flew over forest that grew denser the farther we crossed it. The trees were of such towering height that I thought I could probably lean over the edge of the hovercraft and almost touch their spires. The green of this forest was spindled, and the hues were so deep a green it almost appeared blue.

The smell was so rich and crisp, I wanted to collect it in a receptacle and carry it home to fill my dwelling with.

"What are these trees?" I asked over the wind.

"Picea," he responded, the wind carrying the answer back to me. "Pinus, which is of the same family. Abies as well, and perhaps Cedrus. All part of the Pinaceae family. They are all conifers."

I breathed in so deeply it made me feel lightheaded. It also sparked my curiosity.

"Do you have a sense of smell?"

He did not look toward me, but he tilted his head as if in thought. "I can engage olfactory mechanics if I choose, so affirmative."

"Engage them now," I encouraged. "I have never smelled anything as wondrous as this."

If he obeyed, he did not say so.

As the rich scent of the forest below us grew, the temperature dropped until there was a distinct chill in the air. I activated the settings on my jumpsuit to conform to the descent in temperature, adding gloves for my hands, a scarf extension around my neck, and a cowl I tightened over my head to secure it against the shove of the wind.

I eyed Seven's broad back and wondered if he felt heat and cold. Given that he had not responded to my command for him to sniff the air, I refrained from asking him if he felt the bite in the air.

There was no thinning of the trees. It was an instantaneous change. One moment we were flying over dense forest, and in the next, we were above exposed land covered in low-lying shrub and rocks. The earth stretched north as far as I could see until it erupted into the sky in a range of jagged, dark mountains. A wide river curved through the land like a great serpent of old.

The hovercraft descended in altitude until Seven landed the vehicle on a barren stretch of rock.

"Do you test all of the water on the planet for life forms?" I asked, as I clambered down from the hovercraft.

"Affirmative," he said. "But I am but one member of an entire team."

The ground here was different. The sand of the oceanside

had shifted and sank underfoot, making it feel as if I were fighting to gain every step. The landscape here rolled underfoot, the rocks loose, the shrub grasping for my boots. I scrambled after Seven, envious of the length and surety of his stride.

The wind was stronger here on the ground, sweeping dirt and ice crystals into our faces.

"Do you need your goggles back?" I asked, raising my voice for my words to reach him where he strode ahead of me. I loosened the straps and pushed them up my forehead, squinting against the wind-driven grit.

He stopped and turned back, waiting until I reached his side. I moved to pull the goggles over my head and offer them to him, but his hand on mine froze me in place.

Even through my gloves, I could feel the coolness of the Tivadium.

"Keep them in your possession," he said. He stunned me even more by tugging the goggles down over my eyes and adjusting the straps until the fit was comfortable. "Human eyes are far more easily damaged than mine."

I stared after him for a long moment as he forded a path through the low-lying, coarse shrub to the river's bank. I shook myself out of my stupor and hurried after him.

The river's edge was different from the ocean's and even from the marsh and lake we had visited. The shore of the river was made up of rock rather than sand or mud. The rocks were almost as numerous as the sand, small, rounded pebbles in varying shapes, sizes, and colors.

I knelt and retracted my glove. I grasped a handful, rolling them in my palm, feeling their weight and admiring their smoothness. I let all of the pebbles fall from my hand save for one. It was the smoothest, its edges worn round by the ceaseless caress of the water. The color was striking, a beautiful, deep gray that seemed dull at first glance until you tilted it in the sunlight and caught the gleam of marbling in the stone.

I glanced at Seven's back where he stood at the water's edge. The color reminded me of the hue of his originally constructed parts.

"Human," he said, and the quiet note in his voice halted me when I would have corrected him. "Come. Look."

I straightened, and, sliding the pebble into a pocket in my jumpsuit and reactivating my glove, I moved to his side.

"What is it?" I whispered.

He dipped his head toward the foothills that skirted the jagged peaks. "Just there. Do you see them?"

I peered in the direction he indicated but saw nothing that would have captured his attention. Nothing within a human's range of vision, at least.

"How far out am I looking?" I asked.

"Almost ten kilometers, roughly," he said.

I turned and gaped at him. "No human could possibly see that far, even with a powerful pair of optical lenses." I twisted back to the vista before us. "I couldn't even see fine details a kilometer out."

I heard a click and a mechanical whirring behind me, and then he reached over my shoulder.

"Here," he said. "Use this."

I took the device from him. It resembled an optical lens, though it was dark in color. I held it to my eye and pushed a node on the side. The lens lengthened, sharpening my vision to incredible distances.

I could make out the finest details on the pebbles on the opposite riverbank. I could see the blue sparkle of sunlight on the snow veiling the highest peak.

"What is this?" I asked, awed by its power.

"My ocular device."

I almost dropped it. "This is your *eye*?" I glanced up at him, and indeed, where his right eye had been, there was now an empty socket gaping at me. My stomach lurched.

"Affirmative."

"Mother of cybernetics. Seven, you do *not* just hand someone your eyeball without a little warning."

"My apologies," he said. "When I next remove something from an orifice for your benefit, I will inform you thusly."

I stared at him for a long moment, wondering if he was teasing me. He did not strike me as a robot to have humor programmed into his database, but then again, he had told me a funny story to distract me from a panic episode.

"You do that," I said, voice wry.

Before I turned away, I could have sworn I saw his face plates shift into a smile.

"Where am I looking?" I asked.

His arm extending over my shoulder, and I sucked in a breath at his closeness. "Just there."

I swallowed and held his...eye...up to my eye. I directed the lens in the direction he indicated. It took me a moment to work the focus and see with clarity, but when I did, I laughed in delight.

"Dogs!" I tilted my head back to look up at him. "That is a pack of dogs!"

"They have resorted to their ancestral behavior now and are closer to wolves, but yes."

I peered through the borrowed lens and studied the pack. I scanned slowly and spotted a small cave tucked into the mountainside immediately above the dogs. I kept the lens focused on the cave's opening for long minutes and was rewarded for my vigilance. Small, fuzzy heads tipped with pointed ears appeared at the cave's entrance.

"There's a den with puppies!" I exclaimed.

"Keep your voice down," Seven said quietly as three of the adult canine's swiveled toward me.

I lowered the lens and glanced at Seven. He knelt by the river's edge, siphoning water through his fingertips. "They can hear me even at this distance?"

"Affirmative," he said. "Hear and smell. How many young are there?"

I lifted the lens and focused on the distant foothills. "I count four," I whispered. "But there could be more deeper in the den."

"And the adults and adolescents?" he asked.

I panned the lens across the area, watching four dogs that appeared to be only about a revolution old wrestle and play. I spotted seven adults lying in various positions fanning out from the entrance of the den. There was movement within the den, but the shadows were too deep for me to penetrate, even with Seven's ocular device.

"At least eleven, but possibly twelve."

"The other members of the Druid pack must be out hunting," he said. "Keep an eye on our surroundings. I would not do them much good, but a human would be an acceptable meal."

I glanced at him quickly, but he was studying the data displayed on his forearm. I adjusted the lens and scanned the far riverbank before turning and scanning the forest's edge behind us. I could find no evidence that we might soon be prey, but I edged closer to Seven's formidable form as I trained the lens on the dogs in the distance.

"The Druid pack?" I asked.

"The largest dog pack we have studied," he said. "The pack began with five dogs banding together ten revolutions ago. Our latest records show the pack has twenty-one members now. But that is not counting the young you just spotted."

"That is incredible. How many packs are being studied?"

"Eight, in this ecosystem."

"Do you study them as well?" I asked.

"I watch for packs whenever I am in the field and record my findings to report to the teams who study them."

"Is your eyeball recording what I'm seeing?"

"Affirmative," he said.

I smiled, but it faded as I watched the dogs in the distance. Their ears pricked and then went flat to their heads. Their hackles rose as the adults sprang to their feet and barked at the frolicking youngsters. The adolescent dogs raced to the den, tails tucked between their legs. The adults followed closely at their heels.

"Seven? Something is happening."

I scanned the foothills and plain before them, searching for the threat that had frightened them. I saw no predators, nothing that would have alarmed them.

Unease crept over me when I found nothing that hinted at

their retreat.

I felt the robot's presence at my side. "Do you see anything?" I asked him.

He extended a hand, and I placed the eye he had loaned me in his palm. I did not look away as he screwed it back in place.

He scanned the stretch of land before us, but like me, he must not have found the source of the threat. When he lifted his gaze to the mountains, though, he stiffened.

"What is it?" I whispered, searching the landscape.

The sky had darkened and dense clouds crept over the sun, casting shadows over the land. I looked to the jagged peaks and found them cloaked in heavy clouds that grew denser as they rolled down the mountain.

"Back to the hovercraft," he said, and the bite of command in his words sent alarm racing up my spine. I did not feel fear, though, until he caught my elbow in his oversized hand and began to walk so quickly I was forced to run to keep up with him.

"What's wrong?" I gasped.

I glanced over my shoulder as the sky grew darker. The mountains were obscured by clouds now. I tripped, and his grip on my arm was the only thing that kept me from falling.

"A storm."

the eleventh chapter

THE WORDS SENT A CHILL over me that had nothing to do with the rapidly falling temperatures. The wind that had swept over us before now howled and tore at us, rushing between us so forcefully that I feared if he did not have a grip on my arm, I would have been blown away.

I remembered storms from the time before. I remembered how they had shredded everything in their path, laying waste to the last of the human cities that had stood in ruins after the wars. I remembered hearing the roar and the wail of the storms even deep under the safety of the ground. I remembered how dwellings would rumble and quake as a storm passed over the surface.

I stumbled as a rock rolled underfoot. Pain wrenched through my ankle, and I cried out.

Seven did not even pause. He swept me up into his arms, cradling me against his chest. He ran at a speed that almost rivaled his hovercraft.

When he reached the vehicle, he practically tossed me aboard and leapt up after me.

"Strap yourself in," he ordered, firing up the engine.

I did so with trembling fingers, gaze beyond him on the wall of clouds that approached us with the speed of a hover-rail.

We shot into the sky so quickly and suddenly a scream was torn from my throat. I grappled with the straps around me, securing the harness.

Seven darted a glance over his shoulder at me. "While you

are in my charge, human, I am bound by cybernetics law to not allow harm to come to you," he said.

And then we were flying, retreating from the approaching storm at top speeds.

I looked back, unable to resist. The storm thundered toward us, sweeping like a wave over everything in its wake. Wind buffeted us, tossing the hovercraft violently. Ice stung my face.

We were not going to outrun the storm, I realized.

It barreled toward us with too much speed and force for us to evade it, even in a hovercraft. The storm blocked out the sky and swallowed the earth beneath it.

It happened too quickly for fear to consume me.

The storm swallowed us in a tumult of sound and fury. The hovercraft was flipped end over end. Secured in the harness, I could only scream as I was flung one way and then another. It was as if I were being wrenched apart, and the only thing keeping my limbs from being flung in opposite directions were the straps secured around me.

I could see nothing but clouds and ice and snow around me, sharp and cold and stinging. I almost laughed when I remembered my request to fly high enough to touch the clouds.

Pain sliced through me as the hovercraft struck something. Shadows flickered through the whirlwind of the storm, and the violence grew. With it, so did the agony, confusion, and fear, before suddenly, everything went dark.

My head throbbed in time with my heart. My shoulders ached, and my hands tingled with numbness. Cold like I had never felt before bit through clothing and flesh down to the bone.

I was not certain how much time had passed when I finally surfaced from unconsciousness. Pain rippled through me when I tried to move, and a moan slipped from my lips.

The sound startled me in the stark, hushed silence that had enveloped the world. I blinked and stared at my surrounding in confusion.

Everything was white. The ground, the broken shards of the forest, the sky. Awareness flooded back in far more swiftly than consciousness.

I was hanging upside down. I lurched, flailing in panic, but the jumpseat's harness held me securely in place.

The remnants of the hovercraft creaked and groaned. I froze. I pulled my arms into my chest, rubbing at my skin to ease the sensation of pricks and needling numbness in my hands.

I struggled to take stock of my injuries, but the pain was so all encompassing I could not pinpoint any specific injuries.

I tucked my chin, struggling to lift my head. My borrowed goggles were gone, but the world around me was muted and cast in shadow.

From what I could see, the hovercraft was snagged precariously by the trees. The canopy of the trees around that were not snapped in half towered above me. The wings of the hovercraft were shredded off, part of the nose and tail were gone.

I tried to call out, but my voice was a silent croak. I had to swallow numerous times before I could force sound through my lips.

"Seven?" I cried, but there was no response.

He was nowhere to be seen.

I tilted my head back and peered at the ground. I could not be certain with the blanket of white, but I thought I was caught about four to six meters off the ground.

I shifted carefully, and the hovercraft lurched with a groan, sliding lower in its snare. I clutched the straps holding me in place, but the descent was snagged with such force my neck cracked.

I had to get free before the hovercraft plummeted the rest of the way to the ground. There was enough of the vehicle left that if it fell with me trapped under it, I would be crushed.

As my awareness grew, so did the cold. My fingers fumbled with the buckles of the harness, clumsy and slow and numb.

This fall was going to hurt. If I landed wrong, it could kill me. But I would die if I stayed here. Either from the cold or from being crushed when the remnants of the hovercraft fell.

I twisted one arm through the straps, locking my fingers as tightly as I could. Then I slowly worked the last clip of the harness holding me securely in place.

Even though I knew it was coming, the sensation of falling made me cry out in panic. That cry turned to a yelp of pain when I was yanked to a halt mid fall by the binding around my arm. My shoulder bore the brunt of it, and for an instant, I thought the weight of my body would tear the socket apart. The strap dug into my wrist, burning and cinching so tight I was afraid my wrist would be severed.

I had underestimated how heavy I would feel held with only one arm. And I had overestimated the strength of my grip.

I scrambled to hold on, kicking my legs with the effort. My nails tore and my fingers wrenched painfully as I lost my grip on the harness strap. The strap tore across my palm like a blade of fire as it slipped through my grasp.

THE SNOW CUSHIONED my landing, but it was still enough of a blow to drive the breath from my lungs and sight from my eyes for long moments.

A groan above me had my eyes straining to focus. I had fallen flat on my back, and I had a perfect view of the trees above me buckling under the weight of the hovercraft. It groaned again, jolting and creaking.

Breath still evading me, I rolled to my hands and knees. The sudden movement almost made me black out, but I grit my teeth against the pull of darkness and scrambled through the snow. I crawled frantically, fighting against the powder that moved like sand under me.

There was a scream of metal and the crack of timber above me.

I flung myself to the side as the hovercraft crashed to the ground. I braced my arms around my face and over my head as a plume of snow, metal shards, and wood debris swept over me like a wave.

A tremor that had nothing to do with the cold swept over me as I sat up and brushed snow from my face. The hovercraft had landed exactly where I had fallen, the edge of twisted, warped metal less than a meter from where I cowered.

I could not breathe. I choked and gasped, struggling to draw air into my stuttering lungs. When I finally managed to gulp down a lungful of air, it sounded caught between a sob and a wheeze.

I huddled in the snow and trembled as adrenalin ran its

course through my system. I pressed my hands against my chest and peered at the forest around me in a daze.

The woods were deep and dark in the wake of the storm. There was silence all around me, made even quieter after the voracious howling of the wind that seemed to still ring in my ears. Debris from the forest and the hovercraft were scattered all around me.

I tilted my head back and peered at the sky. The canopy above was tattered, the trees splintered and shorn. What I could see above me was gray, the clouds sagging against the shards of treetops as if the shattered trunks were holding up the weight of the sky.

Looking up made me dizzy, and as the last surges of adrenaline faded, I was able to take stock of my own state. My jumpsuit was torn in places, revealing skin that was cut, abraded, and leached of color from the cold. Several of the cuts were deep and ragged, and they bled freely. But none penetrated my skin to the bone, and none appeared to be life threatening. I was battered and bruised but not grievously injured.

Even upright, my head throbbed in time with my heart, and the forest around me spun and shifted. My ankle ached so sharply I did not attempt to stand. I crawled closer to the wreckage of the hovercraft and leaned against its remains.

Time must have bled away from me, because when I blinked, the forest was darker. The cold bit down into my bones. I was stiff with it and with stillness. I lurched into wakefulness. A fine blanket of snow covered me.

I had to stay awake. I knew if I gave in to the urge to sleep, I would never awaken.

Frantically, I scrambled upright and almost pitched face first into the snow when my ankle gave out. Pain flared like a flame through my leg, driving out the numbness that had crept over my limbs. The pain brought with it a jolt of awareness.

"Seven?" I called. I raised my voice and shouted his name, but the deep snow muffled the sound.

I had to find him.

I took a step and fell as soon as I put weight on my right foot. I cursed, spitting out snow, and rolled into a sitting position. Even through the thick insular fit of my boots, I could see the swelling. I did not take my boot off to examine the damage. I was afraid I would not be able to force my foot back into its confines.

I crawled to the downed hovercraft and clung to the edge as I pulled myself to my feet. I trembled violently as I forced more and more of my weight onto my injured ankle. Panting, I clenched my teeth to keep from crying out.

There was no way I would find Seven or make it out of the forest if I could not walk. Sweat trickled down my back as I took the first, agonizing step, and I clung to the mangled edge of the hovercraft. A sob escaped me despite my best efforts as I hobbled the short distance to the edge of the shorn off wing.

Leaning against the vehicle, I scrubbed the back of my wrist across my cheeks. Already I could feel the prickling burn of the tears freezing against my cheeks. I started to shiver again now that I was upright and moving.

I looked up at the darkening sky and then studied the treetops. From the damage to the canopy, we had not fallen straight out of the sky. We had plummeted into the forest at an angle, tossed over the treetops like the ships I had seen in old holovids were battered and manipulated by the waves.

All around me, I saw nothing but the immediate damage of the hovercraft and the deep drifts of snow. The debris field lay beyond.

I tested my weight on my ankle. The pain was knife-like, sharp and grating. It swept fire up my leg, but my ankle did not buckle beneath me. I straightened away from the hovercraft and took one hobbling step after another.

The debris field led me like a trail through the forest. I had never seen snow before, but I recognized it from the old records. The storms I had known were ones of dust.

The snow behaved much like sand, shifting and changeful underfoot. The technology of my jumpsuit kept me dry and relatively warm, save for the sections of exposed skin the torn fabric revealed. The cold had at least slowed my bleeding.

The snow was wet and heavy. In places, the drifts were waist-deep. Closer to the base of the trees, the snow was more shallow, up to my knees in some places, only ankle deep in others. The tree trunks and limbs gave me something to hold onto when I wobbled unsteadily, my ankle buckling under me.

"Seven?" I called as darkness began to descend over the forest. There was no response.

I waded through the snow following the debris field away from the wreckage. Small splinters of metal, shards of different sections of wings and tail, and chunks of the hovercraft as long as I was tall littered the forest floor, half buried in the snow. Fragments of trees, snapped in half with the bark peeled off, and the blue-green needles of their foliage were spread out amongst the debris.

I searched methodically and then, as the darkness

deepened, frantically.

"Seven!" I called, even though I did not know what might be lurking in the forest to hear me. "Seven! Where are you?"

The cold dulled my senses, exhaustion and fear and pain making me slow to react when I heard the low groan nearby.

"Seven!" I yelled, and snow fell from a laden branch at the volume. "If you can hear me, answer me!"

"Human," a low voice rasped.

I tried to run toward the sound, but my ankle gave out with a flair of agony so bright, my vision went dark. I did not try to stand again. I knew there was no use. I sobbed a curse in frustration.

"I'm coming, Seven. I'm coming."

I crawled through the snow. In holovids, I always thought snow looked beautiful, even decorative. At the moment, though, hands becoming more numb by the moment, I hated it.

I found Seven beneath a piece of the hovercraft's wing. Only his head and one arm were visible. I scrambled to his side and reached for the broad plate of his face. One side of his head bore a deep dent. I paused and retracted the glove of my jumpsuit before I gently touched the squared angle of his jaw. The metal was as cold as the snow that surrounded us.

"Seven?" My voice trembled. "Can you hear me?"

There were no lids on his eyes, but I heard a shifting of the optics in his eyes as he focused on me. "Your yelling could be heard halfway to the Citadel, human," he said.

A laugh that sounded like a sob escaped me. "We can only hope. We need help."

"I activated the emergency beacon before we went down,"

he wheezed.

I rested a hand on his exposed shoulder. "Are you hurt?"

"I believe I bear some damage and am malfunctioning." His voice was labored and even more hollow than usual. "Have you sustained damage?"

The courteous formality of his voice made me sag with relief. Only now that I was by his side did I allow myself to acknowledge how frightened I had been. "I bear some damage as well, but not too much." I examined the wing pinning him to the ground. "Let's get this off of you. Can you help me?"

We shoved and heaved the massive weight up until Seven could drag himself from beneath it.

I sucked in a breath as he pulled himself free. The Tivadium of his arms was whole and unscathed. The rest of his body had sustained damage, just as he said. His chest was caved in and cracked, but the worst damage was his legs. My stomach lurched. One leg was ripped away entirely just above the knee joint, exposing wires and gears and hardware. The other leg was twisted and bent so far out of its usual angle that I knew he would not be able to stand.

"Oh, Seven," I whispered. "Does this..." I reached out toward the gaping, bloodless wound of his severed leg but did not touch it. "Do you feel this? Does it hurt you?"

"I feel a degree of discomfort, but physical pain is not a sensation my systems recognize."

"*Good*," I said.

Night was falling, and the shadows deepened.

I sucked in an uneven breath and met Seven's gaze as he struggled into a seated position. I caught his arm to stabilize him, and I thought the expression on his face was one of surprise.

"We're not getting out of here tonight," I said.

His head dipped. "You are correct."

"What do we do?" With the encroaching darkness, the cold grew, biting through the material of my jumpsuit. "I don't know if we'll survive out here in the forest tonight."

"The odds are not in our favor," he said. "But if we build shelter, we will increase our chances."

I looked around, barely able to see anything in the dark. "The branches kept much of the snow from the bottom of the trees. I think we should build a shelter there." I pointed to the closest one with its branches forming a skirt at its base. I squinted, no longer able to see anything of him but shadow. "Can you form a light?"

There was a soft click like the snap of fingers, and a blue light sprang to life in his palm.

"Will this suffice?" he asked.

"Yes," I said. I had an idea and crawled to the shorn wing of the hovercraft. "This outer shell of material looks as if it is flexible. Or at least thin enough for you to be able to bend it." When he offered no response, I turned back to him and found his head sagging toward his chest. "Seven!"

There was a grating sound and a wheezing in his chest cavity that almost sounded like human lungs struggling for breath.

"I am still in...working order," he said, but his voice was slow and slurred.

"Stay with me," I begged. "I need you."

"I am currently..." The grinding sound came again, accompanied by a wet squelch in his throat. "Incapable of going anywhere."

"Good. Keep talking to me," I ordered. "Stay awake. Can you take this panel off of the wing?"

His head lolled on his neck but he gave me a raspy, "Yes."

I pushed carefully to my feet and hobbled around the trees within the glow of the blue light Seven emitted. I collected fallen branches that were densely packed with needled foliage and piled them beside the tree.

A metallic groan had my gaze shooting to Seven, but it was just the panel being peeled from the wing.

"Can you crawl under the tree here?" I asked.

I had to help him as he dragged himself through the snow. My heart was caught in my throat as the blue glow from his hand glinted on the bolts and screws spilling from his shorn-off leg. I tugged the low branches aside so he could wedge himself into the cloistered space under the tree.

When he was ensconced in our makeshift shelter, the glow of light dimmed. The faint blue gleam was just enough to illuminate my way as I leaned the boughs against the base of the tree. I struggled to ignore how dark the forest was at my back. Strange sounds began to echo through the dark, and I rushed to drag the panel of metal from the wing to the tree.

The thickened drape of limbs created a lean-to structure that would provide shelter against the night. I propped the pliable metal panel over the lean-to I had built, weaving the tree's limbs over it to anchor it in place.

The metal exterior of the shelter blocked all light from Seven. I worked quickly as the night rushed in around me. My neck prickled, and I glanced over my shoulder but could see nothing in the darkness. A creature in the trees called to another. It sent a shiver creeping over me.

I dropped to my knees and crawled to the opening, ducking into the tight space beneath the tree. I breathed a sigh of relief at seeing the gleam of blue light again. Even the air within the shelter felt a few degrees warmer already.

I scooted close to Seven where he leaned against the trunk of the tree. He did not lift his head when I slid into the shelter next to him. I placed a hand tentatively on his wrist, feeling the warmth generated from the light he produced.

It took him long moments to lift his head, and even longer until I heard the shifting of his lenses before his black eyes focused on me.

I swallowed painfully. "How bad is it?"

Gears ground within his damaged chest and some type of fluid leaked from a crack along his side. "By my estimations...I have less than a full day cycle before..." Again I heard the wet squelch of sound. If he were human, I would think he had punctured a lung and was drowning in his own blood. Since he was a robot, I could not even fathom the damage he had sustained. "Before my hardware fails entirely."

"At first light," I said, "we will start for the Citadel. I think I can fashion a sled from the part of the hovercraft."

"No," he rasped. "At first light, you will leave me and head out with the emergency beacon. Assistance will come for you."

I was surprised at the vehement refusal that rose in my chest at the idea of leaving him here alone. He may not feel the cold and pain in the same way I did, but the thought of abandoning him to face a slow, grinding halt of his gears and cogs alone was abhorrent.

I did not waste my energy arguing with him, though. I

curled up at his side, exhaustion and the cold weighing heavily on me. Morning felt as if it were a lifetime away.

I WOKE TO SUCH INTENSE warmth that I sighed and, for a long moment, thought it had all been a dream.

Then I heard the groan of metal and a grinding of gears, and it jerked me back to awareness.

I jolted upright, only belatedly realizing I had been curled up against Seven in sleep with my head resting on his shoulder.

The heat he was putting off warmed the tight interior of our makeshift shelter. It had eased the ache in my bones and the cramps in my muscles.

But he shuddered with it, gears whining audibly.

"What are you doing?"

"Warming you," he said, but his voice sounded strangely discordant.

I eased away from him. "How?" I demanded.

"It is of...no consequence." His words sounded like a gasp.

"Yes, it is," I argued. "Because it is obviously harming you. How are you putting off so much heat?"

He did not answer me for so long that I asked the question again.

"Burning up...my hardware to keep you warm," he said finally, and there was a wheeze to the sound. "I scanned...your system, and your temperature...was dropping...alarmingly."

"Stop it." I scrambled away from him. "*Stop.*"

"Do not...be alarmed," he said. "I told...you...I would keep...you from harm."

"Not like this," I argued. I moved farther away from him. "So help me, if you do not stop killing yourself to warm me, I will crawl out of this shelter and sleep in the snow."

"I cannot be...killed," he rasped. "I am...a machine."

"You may not die as a human does, but you *can* be destroyed," I snapped, "and I will not have that. Do not make me freeze to death to stop you."

That airbrake sound came from him. I had heard it before, but only now did I realize it was his version of a laugh. He stopped shuddering, and while the heat still bloomed in the small space, it was no longer pouring off of him like he was a furnace.

I crept back to his side. "Don't hurt yourself for me," I whispered, and my voice broke. "Please."

"This is a...decommissioning...injury," he labored to say.

It was. There was no denying that. But I said, "We don't know that. The engineers are able to work wonders now." I tried to smile, but I knew it fell flat. "Look at what they've done with soul harvesting."

When I heard the rasp of him trying to speak, I rested my head on his shoulder. It was hard and unforgiving and infinitely comforting. "Conserve your energy," I said. "We'll need it for the trek tomorrow."

Somewhere in the distance, a dog howled, a mournful, haunting sound that sent a tremor through me. Sleep eluded me as the cold crept back into our shelter.

The hum of cybernetics and the grind of gears slowed beneath my ear until they stilled completely as the first faint light of morning crept through the forest. Seven did not respond, no matter how many times I called his name and tapped my palm against the plates of his face.

I scrambled out from under our shelter. I was stiff with

the cold and with the all encompassing ache of the beating my body had taken in the crash. The worst pain was centralized in my head and my ankle. When I made to stand, my ankle would not hold my weight.

I fell to the ground no matter how much I tried to grit my teeth through the stabbing agony. It was no use. I could not walk.

"Please, please, please," I whispered when I wanted to scream it.

The sky was a blue so bright it pierced my eyes when I looked up. The temperatures were even colder than they had been last night, and the overwhelming urge to crawl back into the shelter and sleep had me swaying where I knelt.

I did not think I could move Seven far, and even if I could, I had no directional reference to inform our escape from the depths of the wilderness. I could easily head farther away from the Citadel rather than toward it. That was if I could even walk. I could not put any weight on my leg.

I shoved the protective walls of our shelter out of the way and struggled to drag Seven free. His weight pulled at my shoulder joints and my back as I crawled backward and tugged him incremental centimeter after centimeter. It would have been difficult enough if I could stand, but I could not even gain that leverage.

"Wake up, Seven," I urged. "*Please*. Wake up."

He remained still and silent.

I managed to drag him onto the panel he had torn from the wing last night. I sat at his side, winded and sweating. I pushed the hood of my jumpsuit back and tilted my face to the sky. A chill wind parsed my tangled hair.

We needed to head south, I reasoned. And I needed to find a spot in the dense forest where I could see the sun's slant more clearly to gauge the direction. The gouge the fuselage of the hovercraft had torn into the forest might provide me enough perspective.

I alternated between pushing and pulling Seven. The pain in my ankle made my head feel light and set my stomach to churning. By the time I managed to heave his bulk through the snow to the spot where I had crashed into the forest yesterday, the sun had reached its zenith overhead.

"No," I moaned, staring up at the sun directly above me.

At this angle, the sun was directionless, casting no shadows on the snow.

We had made so little progress and already the day was halfway through its rotation. I would not make it even a kilometer farther before nightfall, especially when I was now forced to wait and watch the sun's path through the sky.

I sagged against Seven, my energy and determination spent. I was damp with sweat, but as soon as I stopped moving, a chill settled over me. I trembled with the force of it and palmed away a tear that escaped to roll down my cheek.

Hopelessness crept over me, as pervasive as the cold. I did not want to die here.

I could stay with the crash site and hope the emergency beacon was still sending out a signal to whatever form of rescue may come.

I could fashion a limb from a tree into a crutch and head south. Eventually I would escape the shelter of the forest, and then there were simply kilometers between the Citadel and where I stood. I would be exposed to the elements, basing my trek on a vague direction that might not be entirely accurate. A few degrees one way or the other, and I would wander until nature won the battle and I was left to deteriorate into a scattering of bones.

I would not be able to take Seven with me if I left, and I could not fathom leaving him. It was not because of the soul tethered tentatively to him now that his gears had ground to a halt and his cybernetics had gone still. I realized suddenly that in all my fear and concern for him, that small remnant of Malcolm he possessed had not even crossed my mind. I had not been worried about Malcolm's soul over the last day. My only thoughts had been for Seven, the robot himself.

I rubbed my forehead and then tucked my hands against my chest. My jumpsuit adapted to the temperature, but the tears in the fabric weakened its structure and warmth. The cuts I had sustained in the wreckage throbbed with heat. The deepest across my bicep and down my thigh had begun to bleed again. I had nothing to bind them with, and the blood felt warm as it trickled down my arm and leg.

I was too tired and cold to think, my mind muddled with fear and uncertainty. Stay or go. Abandon Seven or wait for rescue. I could not decide. I did not want to decide. I only wanted to curl up against him and imagine I was back in my dwelling in my warm sleeping pad. My stomach took the opportunity to make its emptiness known.

If only I had thought to pack a satchel with supplies for being stranded in the wilderness.

I laughed at the thought, but my humor died as I remembered something.

Seven's satchel. He had it with him before the storm

swallowed us whole.

The branches of the trees were too thin to be used as a crutch. They bent under my weight when I leaned against them for support. I abandoned the idea and alternated between hopping and crawling as I searched the crash site. I dug through drifts of snow and searched through the scattering of wreckage until I found his satchel caught in the branches of a tree near where I had found him.

I rummaged through it. Of course, there was no food for someone who did not need to eat. But there was a positioning and navigation system, ropes, and other supplies.

Tentative hope unfurled in my chest.

The bonding agent in the pack was for tears in metal, but I applied it carefully to the worst of my cuts. It burned so badly I grit my teeth to contain a scream, but it stopped the bleeding and sealed my torn flesh for the time being.

Panting and trembling, I slung the satchel over my back, tightened the strap across my chest, and crawled back through the wreckage trail to Seven's side.

I fashioned the ropes into a harness around Seven's chest and under his arms. The loops I tied at the opposite end of the ropes fit in a crisscrossing band over my chest.

I knelt at his side with a hand on his battered chest as I fired up the positioning and navigation system. It was a complex tool but simple to use, and it took me only moments to discern the direction we needed to go. I tucked it into my pocket, adjusted the fit of the ropes around me, and tightened the satchel at my back.

If I did not leave now, I never would.

Decided, I crawled.

The ropes stretched taut, digging into my shoulders and breasts. I grunted and strained with the effort, clawing at the snow and dirt with my hands, pushing with my knees, until Seven slid slowly after me. The strain of dragging him behind me made my muscles tremble and black spots dance at the edges of my vision. Nevertheless, I persisted.

The skin over my shoulders and collarbones quickly became raw with the effort. My knees ached, and my hands grew numb. My gloves tore, and soon so did my fingernails.

"Keep going," I chanted to myself. "Just keep going."

I checked the positioning and navigation system regularly to ensure I stayed on course. I had to stop frequently and dig away the buildup of snow around Seven's shoulders and head.

When the ropes tore through my jumpsuit after hours of friction, they rapidly burned through my skin as well. I paused long enough to slather the bonding agent over the tops of my shoulders and across my collarbones. Pain outweighed death.

I sank into the pattern of crawling and cycle of pain. Hand, knee, strain, tug, hand, knee, strain, tug. The burning sensation in my muscles had flared into a conflagration. I trembled with the effort and pressed on.

So entrenched in my infinitesimal progress, it took me long moments to recognize the sound for what it was. The distant hum of a hovercraft brought my head up.

Breathing hard, slick with sweat, I untangled myself from the rope harness and pushed upright with the aid of the tree at my side. The effort to stand had me groaning in pain, but I blocked everything out but the sound.

I searched the sky but saw nothing. The hum of engines grew louder, though, and suddenly a trio of hovercraft passed overhead.

"Here!" I shouted and waved frantically. "We're here!"

Realization struck me that they could not see me through the cover of the trees. I yanked the satchel around my chest. I tore through the supplies until my numb, cramped fingers closed around the flair gun.

It took both of my hands to hold it steady as I aimed it overhead. The recoil was minimal when I pulled the trigger, but I still stumbled and went down hard when I unthinkingly put weight on my damaged ankle.

The top of a tree was singed from where it had blocked the burst of light. There was no change in the hovercrafts' course.

"No, no, no!"

I scrambled to my knees and loaded another flair into the gun. I aimed carefully at the open sky between the tree tops and pulled the trigger.

The vehicles banked sharply at the second flair burst apart in fragments of light and red hues. I sagged in relief. I braced my arm over my face as the descending hovercraft sent a tumult of snow into the air and whipped the tree limbs into a frenzy.

"Second Librarian," the first robot to approach said, "you appear to be in need of assistance."

I slumped back against Seven's prone figure and laughed until I sobbed.

the fourteenth chapter

THE VOYAGE TO THE CITADEL passed like a blur, and I did not remember anything of the transport to the engineering facility.

My ankle was broken, and the damage required surgery. I found myself with my own upgrade with Tivadium rods implanted in my ankle. I remembered the hum of attendants around me and the weightlessness when I awakened, but little else.

The infection that set into the wounds I had sustained in the crash ravaged me with a fever. I could recall only vague snatches through the heat, and even those memories were certainly hallucinations. I remembered my grandmother sitting at my bedside singing softly and tucking one of her quilts around me. I remembered Malcolm leaving my bed even though I begged him not to.

And then there was only blissful coolness and a slow climb to consciousness. My hold on it was tenuous in the beginning, and it took me some time before I could grasp it firmly.

When I finally awakened fully, I was told that I had lost a fortnight of time in delirium.

"What of Seven?" I asked frantically. I thought I had inquired about his condition repeatedly when we were first rescued from the forest but had been told I needed to focus on my own healing. The robot gave me a blank look. I clarified, "Citizen 7-24326."

"Citizen 7-24326 is still undergoing reconstructive engineering."

"I want to see him."

"Him?"

I thought there was curiosity in the robot's voice.

"Yes." When it appeared that the engineer was going to argue with me, I said, "I will not leave this facility until I see him."

The robot inclined its head. "Very well."

The marvels of modern engineering meant there was no pain as I walked. Not even a limp lingered. I was unsteady on my feet, though, and weak from the time spent lost in a fever.

The robot caught my arm in a solicitous grip and led me to a different level.

"It has been an honor to work on one such as Citizen 7-24326," the robot said conversationally as it led me through the corridors. "We have not seen a First Division, Warrior Class in some time now. Aside from this individual, they have all been decommissioned."

The robot guided me toward an observation room with a glass panel that afforded me a view of the adjacent operating room. There were other robots in the room already sitting before a holoscreen.

I paid the robots no mind and rushed to the window. My knees almost gave out when I approached the glass and found Seven eviscerated on a table.

"What are you doing to him?" I demanded, whirling around to confront the robot. My fists clenched.

The robot who had led me here studied me for a long moment before approaching my side. "Citizen 7-24326's current state demands decommissioning. The damage sustained is too great. His functioning capacity is only at eight percent."

"But you can save him?"

"We spoke with Citizen 7-24326 at length, and the decision was made to harvest his interior framework and transfer it. Upgrade it."

"You spoke with him? So he's..." I swallowed. "Alive?"

"He is cognizant. We had to restart his cybernetics to ensure the reconstructive engineering was not a wasted effort."

I pressed a hand against the glass. "He's been here the entire time I have?"

"Yes."

"Why is it taking so long?"

The robot clasped its hands, and I could almost interpret the look I caught in the reflection as one of great, long-suffering patience. "Second Librarian, this is delicate work. Made even more so by the fact that much of his hardware is outdated. Most of our engineers have never even seen the rudimentary systems he has in place, let alone worked on them. It is taking so long, because he is in a precarious situation. We are trying to preserve as much of his original cybernetics as we can."

"He has to be handled with the utmost care," I said.

The robot inclined its head. "He has been, and he will continue to be."

They had removed his twisted leg, and I spotted it in the corner of the room. Seeing it propped out of the way, looking as if such a vital piece of him were being discarded, broke my heart.

"You said you are going to upgrade his interior framework. I assume you'll be using Tivadium?"

"Of course."

"But he will still be..." My voice trailed away as I watched the engineers in the room work. Their movements were precise. "Will he still be the same?" Would he still be *Seven*?

"We are preserving as much as we can," the robot said. "This is our most intensive instance of reconstructive engineering where we are transferring so much into a new host. But our engineers are confident."

"I need to see him," I insisted. When the engineers glanced at one another, I said, "I *must* see him."

They did not need to confer long given my staunch insistence that I would not leave until I could be in the room with him.

The operating room was cool and bright, and I approached his side quickly. His chest plate that had been caved in and cracked was removed, exposing the mechanics of his torso. My heart clenched at how vulnerable he looked laid out on the table as engineers moved around him and worked steadily and silently.

I moved around them, careful not to interrupt their work, and took up the space by his head. His dented skull cap had been removed as well, and I could see the faint flashes and flickers of his cybernetics.

"Seven," I whispered.

There was a spark of blue light in his exposed head, and I heard the faint whirring sound of his lenses adjusting. I shifted closer until he could see me without having to move his head.

"Nell," he said, and his voice held none of the resonance it had. It sounded faint and hollow.

I laughed as my vision blurred. I stretched a hand out hesitantly and placed it against the hard plate of his jaw. "I knew you knew my name."

"Affirmative," he rasped. "Are...you well?"

"Yes," I said, keeping my voice soft and my hand on his face gentle. Without realizing it, my hand had begun to stroke along the squared angle of his jaw. "I'm fine. And you are going to be."

"They...told me you...saved me." His chin dipped as if he were looking down at the carnage of his body splayed open.

I moved and leaned in closer, hoping to block out the horrific site of his exterior sliced away. "We saved one another," I said.

The engineers offered no objections when I requested a stool be brought in so I could sit at Seven's side, close to his head leaning over so I filled his vision. I kept my hand on his face as I sat with him. Sometimes I could see the spark of cybernetics in his exposed head. When he was conscious, I spoke to him, and I watched the sound of my voice send a flicker of blue fire through his synapsis. I wondered what those bright flairs meant. Other times, when his black eyes remained still and the hardware in his head remained dark, I hummed softly.

I did not realize I had fallen asleep until a touch on my shoulder roused me. I straightened, alarm sweeping through me when I saw the engineers rolling the table bearing Seven away.

"Where are they going with him?" I asked, panic pitching my voice high.

"Do not be alarmed," the robot said. "They managed to stabilize his internal hardwiring to the point that it is safe to transfer him."

"May I stay with him while they do so?"

"No," the robot said. "It is a dangerous process for humans to be exposed to. But the engineers said you were instrumental in helping stabilize his hardwiring. For that, we thank you." The robot held onto my arm as I eased off the stool. I felt weak and unsteady, and I was reminded that I was still recovering. "It is time for you to return to your dwelling and rest. Recover. I have already arranged for an escort."

I nodded, staring after Seven. "You'll send word about his state?"

"Of course."

I fell asleep on the hover-rail to the second sector. I thanked the robot charged with ensuring my safe trek to my dwelling and entered my home. It was dark, and I quickly activated the lights. My steps dragged as I moved into my sleeping chamber, and the receptacle I carried of my few possessions weighed heavily in my hand.

I dropped everything on the floor and moved in a daze into the cleansing closet, washing away the grime of the wreck and the fortnight of recovery. At the facility, another robot had helped untangle the snarls from my hair, so my head did not need to be shorn. I pulled a detangling device through the short length after washing and donned a night sheath.

My grandmother's quilts seemed brighter than ever after the gleaming, colorless rooms of the engineering facility.

I set my new boots and new jumpsuit aside. I carried the bag to the waste dispenser and tossed my old boots within. The one encasing my injured ankle had required the engineers cut it off my foot. I tugged my torn, stained jumpsuit from the bag and started to toss it into the dispenser after my ruined boots when a slight weight on one side of the garment stopped me.

I felt along the seam of the jumpsuit until I reached the pocket, and memory struck me. The rock I had picked up at the riverside was still in my jumpsuit pocket.

I rolled it between my palms and watched the light draw veins of shimmer out of the dull depths. It was a beautiful stone, subtle and sturdy. I discarded my tattered jumpsuit and carried the stone into my sleeping chamber. I placed the smooth pebble on the table beside my sleeping pad as I climbed beneath my grandmother's quilts.

I commanded the lights off and immediately wanted to switch them back on. I could almost see the dark forest looming around me.

I rolled to my side and forced myself to breathe slowly and evenly, even as my heart tried to take flight in my chest. As my eyes adjusted to the darkness, I could make out the stone's smooth curve where it sat on the table.

I stared at it until my eyes grew weighted.

Just as sleep began to claim me, I realized I had never asked about the state of Seven's borrowed soul.

the fifteenth chapter

WHEN THE FACILITY SENT word a week later that Seven's reconstruction had been successful and he had been released from care, the engineers also shared additional knowledge with me. It was my neighbor who alerted the population authority that I was missing. Her concern had launched the search for me.

I had not seen her since my return. When I went to thank her, her door was ajar. Even though it was midday, it was dark within her dwelling.

"Donna?" I called, pausing in the threshold.

There was no response.

My heart quickened, and dread slowed my steps as I crossed to her chamber.

She looked as if she were sleeping, her hair in its neat plait, her arms at her side.

"Donna," I whispered, even though I knew she would not respond.

I approached her sleeping pad reluctantly. This close to her, I could see the gray cast to her face, the slackness in her features. My fingers trembled as I reached out and touched her hand. The warmth was gone out of her. Her skin was cold to the touch.

I drew back quickly, rubbing my hands together to erase that chilling lack of heat.

I wandered into the outer chamber and moved to the paintings hung on the wall. Without her watching me, I had the freedom to study each in turn. Flowers in vases. Fruit in a bowl. A filmy curtain over a window. A bird on a branch. A bee on a blade of grass.

I moved along the wall and stopped when I came to a painting I had never had a chance to study. It was not the most intricate scene, but the changeful blue and green of the water and the tilt of a boat of old captured me.

I carefully lifted the painting from its holding on the wall and carried it back to my dwelling.

I was lost in thought as I traveled to the ninth sector and approached Seven's door. It opened as soon as I reached it, before I could activate the retina scan.

I took a quick step in retreat at the robot on the other side of the door. Stunned, I thought it was a stranger in his dwelling. I did not recognize the robot as the First Division, Warrior Class I had known.

"It is startling," he said, noting my hesitation at his appearance, and his voice was as deep and toneless as ever. The sound of it had me sagging in relief.

He was still the same daunting two meter height. But the dull, weathered slabs of titanium had been replaced by the sleek, pearlescent Tivadium that occasionally shimmered and lost its opaqueness to give me a glimpse of the cybernetics operating beneath the surface. Where before he had been a bulky, outdated weapon, now he was a towering, sleek work of engineering artistry with all the latest upgrades. The only thing that had not been traded out for a newer model was his eyes. They were as dark as ever. It was a relief to see that familiar, impenetrable gaze.

"It will take some getting used to," I admitted. "Where are we going today?"

Nerves gripped me at the thought of going above the surface again, but staying underground no longer felt like an option.

Weeks passed. When I was not working at the Athenaeum, I was collecting samples and exploring water bodies with Seven. We did not encounter anymore ferocious storms, but each time we ventured from the Citadel, I made certain to carry a satchel with me.

"Today, I have been tasked with going back to the river to the north," he said when I entered his dwelling one day two lunar cycles later.

Anxiety gripped me at the memory of the crash and the hopelessness I had felt in the face of being stranded in the wilderness.

Seven clearly read the emotion on my face. "You do not need to come with me."

"No," I said. "I want to."

Even his hovercraft had been replaced with a newer, faster model. As we sped over the forest, I kept an eye on the sky, but I saw no hint of an approaching storm. I could see no evidence of our crash into the forest, either. Already the wilderness had swallowed the proof of our close call almost as easily as it had swallowed us.

The air felt even sharper and more fragrant than I remembered. The mountains seemed taller and more ruggedly beautiful. The river ran green and swift.

I expected to feel trepidation and fear returning to this place, but all I felt was wonder at the wild, untamed nature of the earth.

I tilted my head back to the sky and sucked a deep breath

of crisp air into my lungs. A band had been tightening around my chest since we returned to the Citadel. It loosened now.

"Do you see the dogs?" I asked.

Seven scanned the foothills below the jagged peaks before unscrewing his right eye with a quick twist and handing it to me. "Same location we saw them last time."

I was proud of myself for not grimacing as I accepted his eye. I lifted the lens and focused on the distant foothills.

The puppies were out of the den, and I could see there were actually six, instead of the four I had seen last time. I laughed as I watched their antics. They rolled and tumbled and pounced on one another. As I searched the area, this time I was able to spot seventeen members of the pack.

I watched the pack interact with one another while Seven collected water samples.

"I brought something to show you," he said suddenly.

I drew my gaze from the dog pack. "To show me? What?" I took one last glance at the puppies and then offered him his eye.

I thought he seemed almost hesitant as he collected his satchel and rummaged within. I watched his face as he withdrew something from the pack and thrust it toward me. This new face was so much more mobile than his old one.

My gaze fell to his hands, and my jaw dropped.

"What..." I lifted it carefully from his hands. "How on earth did you get your hands on this?"

"My first job after the war was salvage," he explained.

I held the book as if it would break in my hands. My breath was snared in my chest as I gently opened the cover and turned the pages. "Seven, this is beautiful. I have never actually seen one before."

"It is yours."

My gaze flew back to him. "This is a priceless artifact."

"It is a story meant to be enjoyed," he said. "I thought you would like this author. Her name is Jane Austen. I have a translator you can have to read it."

I ran a hand along the spine. "This is the loveliest thing anyone has ever given me. But...why?"

"You have been sad," he said.

I looked up at him. "How could you tell?"

"I have been recording your facial expressions to study and learn them."

I was not certain how to respond to that curious admission, so I explained, "My neighbor died in her sleep after I was released from the engineering facility. I learned she was the individual who noted my absence and alerted the population authority to search for me."

"Were you friends with this neighbor?" he asked.

"No," I said. "Not really. Our lives had only just intersected, but even so..." My voice trailed away. "I cared about her."

Silence settled and stretched between us, contemplative and comfortable. He was right. I had been sad for the last months, even though they had also been the most enjoyable I remembered living. Donna's death was the easiest explanation, but there was more to it.

Be honest with yourself, I said sternly.

The truth was, I lay awake at night, wondering at the contentment I felt, struggling to understand why I had never felt such levels of companionship with my husband.

Malcolm and I had lived separate lives, and my home had

only been a temporary one for him. I had loved him, deeply. I was certain of it.

So why then did I find my memories of him slipping away now that I was not consciously clinging to them? Why did I think of a humorous anecdote and immediately look forward to sharing it with Seven when I could not remember laughing much with Malcolm? Why did the idea of convincing Seven he needed to commission a life partner suddenly taste bitter in my mouth when I thought of it? And why did it send a splinter of envy into my heart?

"You humans are such frail creatures with such fierce hearts," Seven said suddenly.

I glanced at him in surprise.

"You love and die so easily," he mused. "You do both with abandon and give so freely of yourselves even though you know your life will not last."

I stared out over the river toward the mountains and cradled the book to my chest. "Do you think robots will remember us? Decades from now, when the last of us have died off, do you think the records of our existence will be preserved?"

"I do not know," he said, and I appreciated his honesty, even though it did not ease the ache in my heart. "To want to remember and recall and preserve...That is a human trait, not one of ours. But..."

It was his turn to allow his voice to trail away.

"But what?" I asked.

He turned to me, and the light of the dying sun gleamed in his dark eyes. With the glow reflected in the depths of his gaze, I could almost imagine it was emotion. "But I will remember *you.*"

THE COMM DEVICE TURNED blue after it scanned my retinas, and the doors slid apart. Seven was not on the other side waiting for me, nor was he anywhere in the front room of his dwelling.

I stepped within, gaze drawn to the other side of the room.

The door I had never seen beyond was ajar.

"Hello?" I called. "Seven?"

There was no response as I crossed the room. I lifted a hand to slide the door aside but hesitated.

"Seven? Are you in there?"

Silence met my query.

With a glance over my shoulder, I slipped over the threshold.

I stopped in my tracks, stunned. I had entered another world.

While the exterior room had been barren and featureless, void of any color or comfort, this room was a profusion. It was easily three times as large as my dwelling. The sleeping pad was adorned with colorful, textured blankets. Massive paintings done in a range from the deepest blues to the palest along with greens and grays and whites decorated the walls. I moved unerringly to the paintings, studying the details of the brushstrokes until I realized the subject matter: they were close details of the crest of ocean waves.

An easel stood in one corner of the room, but when I crossed to it and moved to face the painting propped on it, I found the stretched canvas blank. The palette that rested on a work bench behind it held a menagerie of pigment, but when I touched it, I found the paint dry and cracking.

The paintings hung on the wall were breathtaking, but the rest of the room commanded my attention. One wall was dominated by a floor to ceiling bookcase. My jaw dropped as I crossed to it and ran my hand along a shelf. These were not holorecords but true books made of paper and wood and leather.

On one shelf, propped between books, was a piece of titanium. I recognized the dented curve of Seven's decommissioned skull.

I touched it with a gentle finger and then turned back to the books. Some were battered, tattered to the point that I was leery of touching them lest they disintegrate. But I could see how carefully he had worked to maintain the integrity of the books. There was a work bench in front of the long stretch of shelves laden with all the accoutrements of preservation.

I had been using the translation device to read the book he had given me, and suddenly that gift felt all the more precious.

A grand piano was the centerpiece of the opposite side of the room. How it had even been moved into the space was beyond me. The black of it gleamed, and no dust coated the ivory keys. I depressed one gently, too gently for it to ring with sound. The sheets of music contained handwritten scribbles and markings that I could not interpret.

All along I had been searching for a spark within him that hinted at my husband's soul. A flair of human likeness that gave testament to the once human spirit residing within him.

And this was it. A sanctuary he kept carefully hidden.

The lighting was soft like sunlight in the morning in the

room, and it gleamed off of something on the table beside his sleeping pad. I glanced toward the doorway, but it remained empty.

I crossed the room and lifted the object. It was heavier than I anticipated. The smooth, rounded container was made of the purest Tivadium. The urn was beautiful.

"What are you doing?"

I almost dropped the urn. I bobbled it and clutched it to my chest as fear slipped through me like a shadow in my veins.

I had imagined human emotion behind his voice on countless occasions, even though his tone and cadence never changed. But now, the thread of danger in his voice raised the hair at the back of my neck. I carefully placed the urn back on the table, straightening its position to match exactly how it had been before I lifted it.

I turned slowly and clasped my hands to keep them from shaking.

"I'm sorry," I said, struggling to keep my voice steady. "I should not have entered your room uninvited."

"No," Seven said slowly. "You should not have."

He stood in the doorway, and for the first time, I saw him as the weapon he had originally been engineered as.

I swallowed. "Why did you hide this from me?"

"I did not hide it from you," he said, voice so tonelessly even that it sounded all the more angry. "I did not invite you to see it. There is a difference."

"Friends share things with one another," I tried.

"And a true friend understands boundaries," he snapped.

I could not argue with that, but I also could not grasp why he had not told me of these treasures when he had to know I would have loved to see them.

"You're right," I said softly. "I should not have entered without your invitation. But I don't understand why you would not have shared this with me."

"Because it means nothing," he said.

"How can that be when you—"

"It means *nothing*!"

He roared the words, and I stumbled backward, my hip slamming into the corner of the table. The force with which I clipped the edge knocked me off balance and I fell, cracking my head against the wall.

Pain burst through the back of my skull. Darkness encroached on my vision. I blinked, struggling to clear my vision.

Seven crouched in front of me, and when he reached for me, I recoiled, flinching and bringing a hand up to shield my face.

He froze when I cringed away from him and eased his oversized bulk to the floor.

"Nell," he said, and his voice was as gentle as I had ever heard it. I squinted at him, stunned to hear my name from his mouth when he still resorted to mainly calling me *human*. "Forgive me. I would never hurt you."

"I know," I whispered.

This time, when he reached for me, I held still and bowed my head as he carefully parted the hair at the back of my head and inspected my scalp.

"You are not bleeding," he said.

I caught his hand as he eased away. My head ached, pain, like ripples, crawling along my scalp from the epicenter where

I had struck the wall. Clutching his hand anchored me when it felt as if my head would tumble right off my shoulders.

"Tell me why it means nothing."

He did not break the grip I had on his hand as he shifted until he leaned against the wall beside me.

"It once meant something," he admitted. "It once meant...*everything*."

We sat shoulder (mine) to elbow (his) against the wall. The sharp pain reverberating in my skull faded, and I studied the paintings hung around the room. The paintings seemed to capture the movement of the water, the shape of light on the waves. I almost expected to feel the dampness of sea foam.

"Malcolm loved music and art," I whispered.

He was silent for so long I thought he would not respond. Finally, he said, "After his soul was tethered to me, I found myself wanting things I had never had any comprehension of or appreciation for."

I looked up at him but he was staring at the piano.

"I wanted to hear music, when once it had been mere cacophony. I wanted to look at art, even though I would have told you before that it was a pointless endeavor." He tapped a finger restlessly on the Tivadium curvature of his thigh. "It was as if I were living a half life and suddenly I was complete. I could not discover enough about your human endeavors."

"When did you turn to creation instead of just consumption?" I asked, because painting souls was a far cry from looking at a work of art. Playing the piano and writing music was vastly different from listening to sound bytes.

"After I gained a companion."

My heart dropped in shock. "What?"

He nodded. "My companion changed things. I felt more. Deeper. The world was bigger. And the rest was no longer enough. I wanted to...be part of it. And participating in creation..." He fell silent, and his fingers still *tap, tap, tapped* away at his thigh. The movement created a small, tinny echo.

I placed my hand over his, stilling the fidget.

"It flayed me open, and it made me something *more*. More than a machine. More than a weapon."

It made you human, I thought. But I did not say the words aloud, and as soon as I thought them, I questioned myself.

Was humanity something as simple and complex as a soul? Were empathy and art, courage and generosity, compassion and inspiration something solely possessed by humans?

"Where is your companion now?" I asked.

He reached over my head and gently lifted the urn. He placed it in my lap, the weight heavy and cool. "Right here," he said, voice as soft as I had ever heard it.

I cupped my hands around the smooth edges and looked up at him. "I don't understand."

"He only lived thirteen revolutions." His tone was hollow. "For all our advancements in science, we still have not been able to stop death."

"How..." I did not understand. A life partner he commissioned would have been as free from the constraints of death as he. "Your companion was a child?" I asked.

There was that grating sound, like gears grinding together in the back of his throat. "A dog. My dog."

"A dog," I whispered, cradling the urn in careful hands.

"And I..." The tapping on his thigh started again, but this time I did not quell it. "I had seen much death in all my revolutions. But none..." He met my gaze, and for the first time I saw something in those dark, fathomless depths. Pain. "None touched me. None rent me in pieces."

My eyes blurred. Of course. Of course he would have no concept of loss when decommissioning was part of a robot's existence. Life did not end when their body's usefulness did. They were transferred into a better, more advanced shell.

How much more viciously would loss sting when one was finally able to comprehend the bitter, agonizing moats of grief?

"I could not bear it. The sorrow of losing the very creature who had taught me what it was to love. Who had shown me unwavering loyalty. Who made me understand the solace of companionship. I wanted..." His voice grated. "I wanted none of it after that." He looked at me. "I gave it back."

MY FINGERS CLENCHED on the cool curves of the urn. "I don't understand."

"I returned the soul to the Athenaeum."

"No." I shook my head. "No, that's not possible. That is not *done*."

"It is," he said. "I made my case before the tribunal and they granted me the right to return the soul I had earned."

"That's not what the holorecords state." My voice was rising, and with it, heat bloomed in my chest and spread upward into my throat and face.

"The records are wrong," he said.

I set the urn gently aside and then scrambled to my feet to face him. "No."

He looked up at me. "Yes."

"*No*," I insisted, and it sounded like a sob. "You have to have his soul. You must!"

He cradled the urn in his palm and slowly rose to his full height. "I returned your husband's soul to the Athenaeum seven revolutions ago."

I pressed a shaking hand to my mouth and stiffened my knees to keep them from buckling. "Why—"

He gestured to the easel, the piano, and the shelves of books. "After I returned the soul, there was just...nothing. I could still paint. I could still read. I could still play. But the joy and fulfillment were gone."

"Because you're not human," I snapped. "And you just tossed aside the one thing we have left of ourselves. The one thing I—" I bit off the scalding words that clamored for release. "You have no understanding of what it is to see your end looming closer and closer and feel this…" I pressed a hand to my chest in a paltry attempt to keep my heart soldered in one piece. "This terror that you'll be the last one, wandering corridors and calling out for people who are no longer there."

"Don't I?" His voice was quiet and even.

We both glanced at the dented skullcap on the shelf.

I turned away, struggling to suck in a breath. "Why did you not tell me?" I whispered. When he remained silent, I glanced at him over my shoulder, hugging myself against the breathless sensation of loss.

"I did tell you," he said. "I told you there would be no commissioning a life partner."

"No," I insisted, slicing the air with my hand. "No, you never once said you no longer possessed my husband's soul."

"What would I have said to you?" he demanded. "The very reason you sought me, the very reason you have offered me your friendship, the very thing you seek, it is not here? Is that what I should have said?"

"Yes!" I shouted the word at him. "You should have said something! Anything! You *knew* why I came to you."

"Did you love him so much then?"

I took a quick step in retreat. "Of course, I did," I said. I could hear the sharpness in my voice, and when his head tilted to the side in that curious way that had always reminded me of a dog, I knew he could hear it as well.

I paced away from him and strode to the piano. I sucked in an unsteady breath and closed my eyes.

His face had faded and blurred over the revolutions, and

his voice was merely a patchwork of sound that I cobbled together and liked to call the memory of the way he spoke. But I could remember his words clearly.

Don't be selfish, Penny, he said, voice cajoling when he left my bed. He knew I hated that nickname. It made me feel as worthless as the tossed aside scraps of copper that had once served as the lowest form of currency in parts of Old Earth. *You know this arrangement is necessary.*

And I did know that. I had known it when I agreed to be his third wife. I had known it when he had taken three more after me. Men were dying off quicker than women, and with only half a dozen births in the last generation, multiple unions were encouraged in an attempt to stave off our declining numbers.

It had not worked. And he did not need to tell me I was being selfish. I knew it, but I could not seem to help it.

I had loved him. With everything I had. But he had never truly been mine, and thankfully, illness had ensured my love had never turned bitter with resentment. It never had the opportunity.

I turned and found Seven standing directly behind me. I took a quick step back, and my hip bumped the keys on the piano, emitting a discordant clang of notes.

"I do not think your love for this human male is what drives you," he said, and if his voice were capable of softening, I thought it would have done so.

"You do not know me," I whispered.

"Erroneous," he said in that toneless, deep voice. "You have shown yourself to me many times now. But I did not know this one thing, and therefore, I did not tell you."

"You didn't know what?" I asked, and though I tried to inject venom in my voice, it came out sounding defeated and tired.

"Would you..." There was a rough grinding sound as if he were swallowing. "Would you have still insisted on showing me what companionship meant had you known?"

It was my turn to remain silent.

"Would you have worked so hard to be my..."

I turned to him when his voice trailed away.

"To be my friend, had you known?" he finished.

I rubbed a suddenly weary hand over my eyes. "I don't know," I said, even though I thought the answer might have been *no*.

"I did not either," he said. "In the beginning, that did not matter. But after...It started to."

I shook my head. "You should have told me."

I left the room that served as a bright, artistic mausoleum to a once vibrant soul and exited the dwelling. I did not allow my tears to fall until I stepped into my own quiet, empty dwelling.

I WENT THROUGH THE motions.

I lay on my sleeping pad during the night, but I did not sleep.

I collected my rations from the food dispensary, but I could barely eat. What I did eat was tasteless.

I went to the Athenaeum, but more often than not, I simply wandered the great halls.

I was adrift. I thought I was familiar with grief, with its aching hollowness and heaviness. But this was different. This was sharp and bitter, like a shard of metal had splintered my chest. The more I worried at it, the deeper it sank into my heart. If I tried to ignore it, I felt its prick at every turn. I could feel it festering, and I had no desire to stop its poisoning from filtering through my bloodstream.

There was almost a revelry to this type of grief. A strange euphoria in it hurting so deeply.

I wondered if this grief was more real than what I had experienced in revolutions past. I wondered if this grief was the culmination of all the revolutions of sorrow I had felt. I wondered if it would always feel this painful, and if so, I wondered if I could bear it.

And what had I lost? I asked myself.

In some ways, it felt as if I had lost my husband all over again. A chance to reconnect with him had been within my grasp, and it had been snatched away.

But I forced myself to be honest.

That was not the driving force of my grief, because I did

not frantically begin the search for his soul anew. I did not even search the records in an attempt to figure out why the return had not been noted in his file. I did not renew my effort to find that last remnant of him.

It confused me, why I had no desire to begin my search anew. I wondered if I had been honest with myself over the revolutions, so I eviscerated my heart and laid it bare. I traced all of its passageways and chambers. I followed its labyrinths into every shadowed corner.

For so long, I had pinned the fate of my own soul to this search. It felt as if it were floating out there now, listless and unanchored with nothing to tether itself to.

With my husband's soul out of reach, where would my soul reside once I was gone? And did it even matter?

I had always thought of my soul as half of a whole, incomplete on its own, roaming with me on this journey toward fulfillment.

And beneath the ache of loneliness and disappointment and fear, I found it. The raw, gaping wound that pulsed in agony. I cared for Seven, and I missed him. Not the receptacle of my husband's soul, the host of what I had sought for so long. *Him*, the robot, the First Division, Warrior Class. The individual who had begrudgingly allowed me to befriend him, and, once I had done so, had given me the world above, friendship, loyalty, laughter. All things that had been absent from my life.

I thought I would show him what companionship was and change his mind about what he needed. But perhaps instead, he had shown me what *I* desperately needed. Not a tenuous connection with the remnants of a soul I had once known and clung to. But a friendship for the *here* and for the *now*. A love and a life in this present moment.

And was that not all I had that I could truly grasp and call my own? Today. This moment.

"Do you have a moment, Nell?"

I sighed at her voice and continued to pretend to eat the ration from my sustenance dispenser. I had no appetite.

The Prime Librarian took a seat across from me.

"Please," I said. "Not today, Marissa."

Instead of a cutting remark or critique, she remained silent for several long moments. Long enough for me to give up the pretense of eating and look at her.

As soon as I did, she smiled. It held none of the hard edges or mockery I had seen in the past. Instead, it seemed almost melancholy.

"Do you know," she said slowly, "when you first started working here, I thought perhaps it was because you wanted to be friends."

I was glad I was not in the midst of swallowing a bite or I would have choked.

"Friends."

She must have heard the bewilderment in my voice, because she chuckled. "Don't worry. You swiftly disabused me of that notion." My brain was too slow to catch up, for she continued, "I quickly realized why you were here, and frankly, I thought it was a phase you would grow out of as you matured."

I stiffened. This had always been a source of contention between us in the thirty revolutions we had known one another.

She held up a hand. "When I realized it was not simply a

grief-stricken whim but an outright obsession, I was torn. I felt both sorry for you and..." She met my gaze. "Envious."

I struggled not to let all the revolutions of resentment and jealousy cloud my view of her when there was no rancor in her tone or face. "Why?"

"I pitied you for spending your entire life searching for a connection to a man who was dead and gone."

I swallowed back the animosity that threatened to choke me when her eyes glazed over.

"And envy that you loved him so much to dedicate yourself to seeking him in the beyond," she whispered. Her smile was sad. "You always were his favorite. And I was so..." She took a deep breath. "So jealous. Especially when after he died it seemed as if you loved him more."

I stared at her, stunned to speechlessness. She appeared to be waiting for a response, but I was too shocked to make my vocal cords work. This time when she smiled, I saw self-recrimination. She stood and moved to leave.

"I was jealous because you were his first," I said. "You were the wife he *chose*, while I was simply one of a number who were assigned to him."

Marissa approached me again, and this time she came around the table and sat at my side.

"I..." I swallowed around the knot in my throat. "I thought I sought his soul because of how much I loved him."

"I'm sure there was some of that," Marissa said.

I nodded. "In the beginning, yes." I met her gaze and admitted the truth that had been plaguing my heart. "But only in the beginning. It's been so long, and we were so young. We were never tempered by life together. So yes, I did love him. But that has not been why I sought his soul for so long. I..."

The knot in my throat was too large to swallow against and too tight for me to squeeze words around.

"You were lonely," Marissa said, voice soft, eyes gleaming once again.

"Desperately," I whispered, and my voice was just a croak. "I've been so desperately lonely. And I've only—" My voice cracked and wobbled, and I had to clench my teeth to keep my chin from trembling. "I've only just realized how I aided my own isolation over the revolutions, and now it is too late."

Her movements were tentative as she reached out and gingerly placed her hand over mine. "It is *not* too late," she assured me. "Do you know..." Her voice was hesitant, and she waited to continue until I met her gaze. "I had never seen you so happy as I had of late."

I considered her words. This truce between us was tentative. I could not consider her a friend over such a brief span of time as our conversation. I would not be unburdening my heart to her any time soon. But as I mulled over her words, I responded honestly.

"I was. I was happy." I sat back with an uncertain laugh. "Happier than I have been in a long, long time."

And in this quiet moment of companionship with a woman I had seen as an enemy from the instant I met her, I could admit something else to myself. Somewhere along the way, it had stopped being a matter of proving to Seven that he would enjoy companionship and it had morphed into simply cherishing every moment we spent together.

The idea of Malcolm's soul being there within my reach had faded when I found myself fascinated with the robot I thought possessed it. It had ceased to be a matter of my soul's destination after I died and more about the soul-deep contentment I felt in Seven's presence.

I did not care where my soul ended up once I was gone, I realized with startling clarity. I would not know.

And my soul...My soul was my own. It was no halfling waiting for its other piece to be complete. It was wondrous and whole, all on its own. And my soul *right now*...That was a different matter entirely. I knew what I needed to do.

I turned my hand under Marissa's until I could clasp her fingers. "I think you and I have never quite understood one another."

She chuckled and squeezed my fingers. "Perhaps we could..."

"Perhaps we could find a way to be friends," I said.

"I would like that," she said softly.

And it stunned me to realize I would like it as well.

THE ENGINEER CALLED another over to join him as I presented the plans I had drafted.

"This is highly unusual."

"I realize that," I said. "But it is within your capability, isn't it?"

"Of course."

Of course. Nothing was beyond their engineering feats. Even tethering a resilient human soul into a being made up of cogs and cybernetics.

It took a full lunar cycle for them to complete the commission, but when they did, it was perfect. I brought it to my dwelling and took several days away from the Athenaeum to spend time with it as it adjusted to its newfound existence.

Marissa visited my dwelling for the first time and marveled at the engineering. We were tentative with one another, uncertain and guarded. But we shared a strange sort of sisterhood. And now that we had cleared the space between us of bitterness, I thought a friendship might well grow and develop.

I spent the day preparing a script in my head for what I would say to him. I formulated and rejected any number of conversations until I finally landed on the words I needed to say to him most.

Please forgive me.

I was uncertain of his schedule, but as the day began, I took care in getting ready. My commission watched me from where it lounged on my bed. It seemed to have a preference for the soft, cushioned surface, and I found I could not discourage it.

I skipped a rationed meal from my food dispensary, knowing the nerves in my stomach were too alight to allow me to eat.

I wiped my palms on my hips. If he were not at his dwelling, I would simply wait until his return. I opened the door, turning to call for the commission, and walked straight into Seven's chest.

I stumbled backward, hand flying up to cup my throbbing cheekbone that had glanced off of him. He caught my arm.

"Forgive me," he said, voice a rumble. "I did not mean to startle you." He drew my hand away from my cheek and studied my face. His features were more mobile now, cloaked in Tivadium instead of titanium, and he frowned. "Or hurt you."

"I'm fine," I assured him, determined not to touch my stinging cheek. "I was actually on my way to see you."

He nodded. "I came here to talk with you."

I glanced toward the open doorway into my sleeping chamber and gestured for him to enter.

We stood opposite from one another, silent and hesitant. It seemed as if a lifetime had passed since I last saw him, and I soaked in the sight of him. Even with his new framework, I could see what a powerful, stalwart figure he was.

I met his gaze.

"Forgive me," he said, at the same moment I said, "I'm sorry."

"I should have told you," he said. "From the very beginning."

"No," I said. "You didn't owe me any explanation. You still don't."

I caught his hand in mine and led him to the resting bench across the room. I darted a glance into my sleeping chamber again, but Seven's gaze did not stray from me. He sat beside me, and the cushion sank under his weight, rolling my knees into his.

He reached out and carefully touched the smarting spot just under my eye. I could tell from the warmth of my skin that I would bruise.

"I'm fine," I assured him and smiled tentatively. "It's nothing."

He shifted, and I realized he was uncertain. "Have you been well?" He glanced at our knees pressed together.

"I've been lonely," I said.

His gaze darted back to mine. "Have you found the individual who truly bears your husband's soul?"

I shook my head, and I chuckled ruefully. "I have not even searched." And I would not.

His head tilted in that way I had always thought was so canine. "Why?"

"Because I..." I swallowed and clasped my hands. "Because I realized it didn't matter. He's gone. He has been for a long time, and nothing I do will bring him back." I looked up at him. "And I finally realized I don't need to bring him back to remember and be at peace with what we shared."

"What about your soul?" he asked, voice pitched as softly as his frame and mechanics would allow.

I shifted closer to him. "I realized something about my soul. I don't need to pin it to something after death. It's here in me now, and it is fine right where it is. It is...It *was* happy. You, your friendship made me happy."

He studied me for a long moment, that midnight gaze searching my face. "I cannot request the life partner you wanted built. I do not have the right without a soul."

I swallowed and risked it all. "But you can choose a partner still, can you not?"

"Choose one." He said the words slowly and cautiously, as if he were not certain what they meant.

"Spending time with you reminded me that the life we have is the only one we humans are truly given," I said, and moisture began to gather in my eyes, despite my firm promise to myself that I would be as rational and logical as possible about this. But fear and hope were an emotionally volatile combination, and my heart was on the line. "I only have one opportunity to live this life. I would like to spend it as your friend and companion. If you would like and if—"

"This would bring me great pleasure," he said quickly.

I studied his features, so strange and new, but the robot underneath was so familiar to me now. "I was using you," I admitted. "I had something to prove to you in becoming your friend, and I did so with an ulterior motive."

"But you did not lie to me," he said. "You shared your motive with me from the beginning."

"It was still callous and manipulative of me," I said. "I never want you to feel like I am your friend simply because I want something from you." My voice cracked at the words, at the reminder of the disservice I had done him. "Can you forgive me?"

"I already have," he said, and a tear slipped from its mooring to spill down my cheek.

I heard a sound from my sleeping chamber. The creak of

stretching joints, the heavy thump as my commission left the sleeping pad.

Seven's gaze swung to the doorway.

"I commissioned something for you," I said as Seven caught sight of it.

He stood slowly, and the pair stared at one another.

"What..." His voice faded with a rough grinding.

I crossed the room and rested my hand on my commission's head. There was no fur to bury my fingers in. No wet tongue to take a swipe at my face. But the tail wagged with the same ferocity I had seen on a dog of flesh and blood instead of Tivadium and cybernetics.

"He won't replace the dog you lost," I said softly, watching Seven's face. "But what I know of dogs is that they want you to continue sharing yourself with another."

He crossed to us slowly, gaze never leaving the canine at my side. The dog's tail wagged harder. "What is his name?"

"Officially, Canidae Companion-1. But I thought you could give him a nickname."

He knelt and extended a hand. The dog left my side and moved past his extended arm to rest his great head against Seven's chest.

Seven met my gaze. "As you gave me the nickname Seven?"

I laughed. "Yes, just like that."

"Nell," he said, and as always, my heart unfurled in my chest at the sound of my name in that deep, toneless voice. "Will you be my friend and my life partner?"

I nodded, pressing my lips together to keep my chin from trembling. "Affirmative."

the twentieth chapter

CITIZEN 19-161015: *twenty revolutions later*

The comm center of my dwelling emitted a tone to indicate someone's presence at my door. When the voice announced the identity of the individual requesting entrance, I scrambled off my resting bench and tucked the book I was reading under the cushion.

When I had awakened from my procedure, the engineer had given the book to me and told me it was a gift from the individual whose soul I had received. I had never heard of such an occurrence before, but I was too intrigued to refuse. I only spoke and read the universal language. It had taken me a number of days to find the code upload for Old Earth's English language. Once I started reading, I limited myself to five pages every day. I had the strangest urge to savor the story. After I reached the end, I would never be able to read it anew again.

I activated the opening sequence to my door, and when the robot ducked its head to enter my dwelling, I was already bowing my head and fisting a hand at my shoulder in respect.

"Citizen 7-24326, it is an honor," I said. "I have never had the privilege of meeting one of the First Division, Warrior Class."

When the warrior offered no response, I lifted my head from its respectful bow. I was stunned to see another robot at his side, though this one stood on all fours. The second robot tilted its head to peer at me and moved its tail appendage in a pendulum motion.

"Is that a canidae?" I asked, and without consciously

deciding to do so, I extended my hand.

"Yes," the warrior said. "His name is One."

"One," I said softly.

As the canine approached me, its tail appendage swayed with even more force. He nudged his head against my hand, and I sucked in a breath. For a moment, the sensation of his cool, smooth head was so strikingly familiar that I felt a whirring of cybernetic pulses in response.

I looked up at the warrior. "I have never seen such a model before, but he is wonderful, Citizen 7-24326."

"He is," the warrior agreed. "He was a special commission. Please, call me Seven."

"Seven," I whispered. I stared up at the warrior for longer than was polite. The depths of the warrior's eyes were so dark that I wondered if I would see the glimmer of stars if I peered into them long enough. I shook off the strange thought. Perhaps I needed to visit the engineers and question them about these sudden occurrences. Nothing in the data I had read indicated side effects.

Everything felt so *bright*. It was a startling sensation, as if I were just waking from sleep mode to a new world in which I did not just *experience* but I also *felt*.

I would venture above the surface to watch the conflagration of the sun rising every morning as if I had never viewed it prior. I would marvel at the pearlescent glint of light on Tivadium and marvel at the delicate beauty of something so strong. I would listen to the storms rolling in from the reawakened seas and wonder at the power and ferocity. I would read a story about love and feel as if the gears and cogs within my chest cavity needed oil.

Sometimes the sensations were so overwhelming, I had to retreat to my dwelling and sit in the dark and quiet.

I had lived through many revolutions and yet everything felt new.

"Are you enjoying the story?" Seven asked, dipping its head toward the book sticking out from under my resting bench cushion.

"It was a gift," I explained. I felt the upward pull of delight on the hardware in my chest cavity when One crossed to my resting bench, climbed onto the cushions, and curled up in the spot where I had been sitting.

"No, please," I said when Seven gestured for the canine to come. "He's fine." His presence felt *right*, as did this warrior calling itself Seven. I could not understand that.

"I—" I searched the central hub in my head to recall what Seven had asked. "I had never seen a book before. And yes, very much. He has too much pride, and she is quite prejudiced. But I think they will discover one another's truths."

Seven was watching me intently as I spoke.

"Have...have you read it?" When its head dipped in the affirmative, I asked, "Do they find one another? In the end?"

Seven tilted its head in almost the same manner of One. I took a step closer to the tall robot and searched its features.

"Forgive me," I said. "I had a procedure done. You see, I recently earned the right to a soul, and I received it just last lunar cycle. The engineers did not warn me of any confusion I may feel as a side effect, but..."

I trailed off, studying Seven and then looking to One.

"I do not believe we have ever met," I said. "I do not recall doing so. But I seem to..."

I searched Seven's features. They were not as delicately made as mine. Even hewn from Tivadium, Seven's features were blunt slabs reminiscent of engineering from an era long ago. There was a brutality in its features, a ferocity. But Seven's chest cavity seemed to go still at my words.

"I feel as if I know you," I whispered. "I know that is not possible," I assured Seven when the warrior remained silent. "But...do you...somehow...know me?"

Seven reached out slowly, and I stood still, frozen in wonder and anticipation I did not fully understand, when its fingers carefully clasped mine. It felt as if a current jolted through me at the contact.

"Affirmative," the warrior said. "And your assumption is correct."

I stared up at Seven, and I heard the thump of One's tail appendage on the cushion of my resting bench.

"They do find one another in the end."

MEGHAN HOLLOWAY FOUND her first Nancy Drew mystery in a sun-dappled attic at the age of eight and subsequently fell in love with the grip and tautness of a well-told mystery. She flew an airplane before she learned how to drive a car, did her undergrad work in Creative Writing in the sweltering south, and finished a Masters of Library and Information Science in the blustery north. She spent a summer and fall in Maine picking peaches and apples, traveled the world for a few years, and did a stint fighting crime in the records section of a police department.

She now lives in the foothills of the Appalachians with her standard poodle and spends her days as a scientist with the requisite glasses but minus the lab coat.

Visit her website at https://www.meghanholloway.com/ or follow her on Facebook, Instagram, or Twitter at @AMeghanHolloway

www.ingramcontent.com/pod-product-compliance
Lightning Source LLC
Chambersburg PA
CBHW061540120726
48001CB00004B/1651